Raven's Son

by

Mary Lee Peck

Author, Mary Lee Peck, earned her Ph.D. in Education from The Ohio State University. Dr. Peck has taught at all levels from preschool to graduate school. Her lifelong love of horses and her experiences with owning, showing, and loving American Quarter Horses inspires her writing. She is the author of T*he Mansion, Breakfast with Friends,* and *Raven's Call.* She has also authored several children's book and a college textbook.

The characters and situations in this book are purely fictional. Any similarity to actual persons or circumstances is purely coincidental.

Published by Reading Research Institute,
Westerville, Ohio

ISBN: 1-931365-06-7
ISBN-13:978-1-931365-06-2

Library of Congress Control No: 2012908786

ACKNOWLEDGMENTS

Special thanks to Helen Hagan and Paula Edwards, who went with me across Texas to gather background information for this book. I am also grateful to Diana Garrison-Lane, Chris Dawson, and Bill Harrison, who served as expert consultants. Watching them train their horses and listening to their comments and stories provided depth to the characters and situations in Raven's Son.

My sister and my husband also deserve my gratitude for listening to the constant re-writes and for offering suggestions and encouragement. Finally, I need to thank Beth Atkinson, who scrutinizes the pre-publication copy for necessary corrections.

Thanks to all of you for your time, support, and direction.

DEDICATION

This book is dedicated to horse lovers everywhere.

Note for the Reader

Raven's Son is a sequel to *Raven's Call*. The action in this second book occurs several years after the events in the previous story. The prologue provides some background information about events in *Raven's Call*.

Raven's Son

by

Mary Lee Peck

Prologue

Jan Taylor-Kendall looked up at the large, round clock inside of the vocal booth of her new recording studio. She turned toward the sound proof window and shielded her eyes, so she could see Roger Allen, her manager, friend, and brother-in-law. "Hey, Roger, I have to wrap this up. I have things to do and places to be," she said.

Roger sighed and shook his head. He glanced over at Tom, the sound engineer, who just threw up his hands and shoved his stool away from the control panel. Roger reached across the controls and pushed the audio button so Jan could hear him. "We need to get this album finished, Jan. It has to get out ahead of the tour."

"I understand that, but it's not going to happen tonight." Jan took off her headset and headed out of the soundproof booth.

Roger met her in the hall. "What's going on with you?" he asked. "Talk to me. Something is wrong; I can tell. I can hear it in your voice when you sing, and I can see it in your eyes right now."

"Nothing is wrong, I promise. You know where I want to

be at sunset when I'm home," she reminded him.

"Is a walk with your horse more important to you than getting this album finished?"

Jan just stared at him.

"Oh, of course it is," groaned Roger. "What was I thinking? Raven is and always will be your first consideration. Poor Brett, I don't know how he puts up with the two of you."

"He loves me," responded Jan quickly. She leaned over and kissed Roger lightly on the cheek. "I'm glad you understand," she said winking at him. "I'll be back bright and cheery at 10:00 tomorrow morning."

She quickly grabbed her bag and headed out of the building before Roger could ask her any more questions. He was much too perceptive, and he knew her too well. By the time she got to her car, the tears that had been choking her all day flooded down her cheeks. *Get a grip*, she admonished. *Tears are not going to solve the problem.*

Despite her effort to control them, the silent tears continued to roll down her face. The disappointing news from Dr. Henderson echoed in her mind. "Sorry, Jan, the results of the pregnancy test are negative again," he had told her. She had tried to sound positive when she left his office, but, in truth, she was devastated. For over a year now, she and Brett had been trying to have a baby. She knew how much he wanted a child, and so did she. Both of her sisters had given birth last year. Lacey and Jim had a boy—Jeremy; and Beth and Roger were the proud parents of a baby girl— Alisha. *Why*, she wondered, *must such seemingly natural things always be so difficult for me? What if I can't ever have a child?* The tears flowed even faster and threatened to blind her. She quickly brushed them aside so she could see the road.

Again tonight, she knew that Brett would try to reassure her by telling her that she was the only family he needed, but she could always see the disappointment in his eyes each time she came home from Dr. Henderson's office with the same bad news.

At last, she pulled down the long, paved drive at the ranch. She drew in a deep breath and could instantly feel the stress start to melt away. Shielding her eyes from the setting sun, she looked out at the long stretch of rocky hills bordering their ranch and her family's Triple Bar Ranch. "I'd better hurry," she muttered as she headed toward the breeding barn. She smiled when Raven's shrill whinny pierced the silence of the cool evening.

Raven, her magnificent black stallion, always knew when she was close and never failed to greet her with his distinctive call. When she was at home on the ranch, he expected her to arrive at his stall door every evening just as the sun was about to set in the huge, Texas sky. It was their special time together—a routine they had been following for more than seven years now.

At sunset, she and Raven used to race across the ridge that stretched along the southern rim of the Kendall Ranch and her family's Triple Bar Ranch as they chased the sun before it slipped beyond the horizon. Together they streaked across the evening sky, relishing in the thrill and joy of their race against time. Uninhibited and fearless, they sped through space, until one, horrible night, a brutal attack by a vicious cougar ended their free-spirited runs. In an effort to protect her from the clutches of the cougar, Raven was seriously injured. As he reared and struck out at the menacing animal, the cougar's sharp claws repeatedly slashed Raven's right foreleg. The battle between the two determined animals continued until Raven's powerful hooves finally struck a fierce blow to the cougar's head and ended the attack.

A large tendon in Raven's right foreleg was severed, and although it eventually healed, he was lame. No longer could he compete in the American Quarter Horse shows across Texas and Oklahoma, but he retired as a World All-Around Champion, and no other horse ever won the title for as many consecutive years as he had. Now he was still the leading stallion in her family's horse breeding program, but there were no more nightly dashes across the ridge to chase the sun. Instead, there were quiet walks along the long, white rail fence of Raven's private paddock.

Raven's value as a stud remained unquestioned even after his accident. He had balance; he had beauty; and his conformation was as near perfect as that of any American Quarter Horse. His long, sleek neck and proportioned, proud head provided the perfect balancing arm for his massive chest and barrel. His angled shoulders served as powerful shock absorbers able to support the weight and impact the front legs of horses experience while running and jumping. The perfect angulations between his shoulders and front legs lengthened his stride and allowed him to cover more ground in a shorter amount of time.

His front and hindquarters were perfectly balanced. A vertical plumb line was apparent from his hips straight down to the ground, intersecting with his hock and his fetlock. He was truly a magnificent representation of the conformation sought by quarter horse breeders and by trainers of race and competition horses.

"Hey, fellow," said Jan, offering Raven a peppermint as she slid open his stall door. "How's my best buddy?"

Raven reached out, quickly grabbed the peppermint, and nickered softly. She lifted his head and gently kissed him on the bridge of his nose. "Are you ready for our walk?" she whispered. Running her hands across his muscled shoulders, she paused over the four streaks of white on his side—another painful reminder of their attack by the cougar. Raven was jet black except for the scars left by the cougar's claws on his left side. The hair over the scar tissue grew back as streaks of white, leaving a strange tattoo on his otherwise perfectly sculpted, jet black torso.

She opened the Dutch doors at the back of Raven's stall, and he followed her out into his private paddock. She didn't need a lead rope or a halter on Raven. Their partnership was so strong he automatically walked beside her, keeping pace with her stride. As they walked along the fence line of the paddock, Jan hummed the melody of one of her new songs she would be recording tomorrow. Although there was an obvious limp in his gait, Raven moved gracefully to the rhythm of the song. At the end of the long, lush paddock, Jan turned toward the western sky. "There it goes, Raven," she said as the sun began to sink behind the ridge and cast a radial spectrum of orange across the cloudless sky.

Raven lifted his head and let out his piercing, high-pitched call as if he were bidding farewell to the blazing sun. And then there was just the silence of nightfall. Jan slid her hand slowly along Raven's injured leg and gently massaged it. She desperately wished she could heal it, so he could run and play as he used to.

After several minutes, Raven gently nudged the top of her head. "Are you ready to go back, Raven? It's supper time in the barn, isn't it? You're such a smart and sensitive animal, my friend," she said as she stood up and draped her arm around his long, sleek neck. "No other horse is as brave and as smart as you are, but some of your offspring are going to give you a run for your money, especially your namesake, Raven's Son. I've heard he's as fast as a speeding bullet—just like you were. Unfortunately, though, he also has your obstinate disposition. So far, he stubbornly refuses to let even the most experienced jockeys ride him. Brett is bringing him home tomorrow for one last try at training him."

She heaved a long sigh as she thought about how disappointed Brett was about the inability to get Raven's Son trained. He was looking forward to having a horse ready to race in the All American Futurity, but he was running out of time to complete the training and pre-racing requirements before the May deadline. Every trainer who tried to work with Raven's Son arrived at the same conclusion—he was too wild to train for racing. Brett's last chance to launch into Quarter Horse racing depended on Tom Blake, a friend who used to train Quarter Horses sometime ago and who agreed to bring Raven's Son here to the ranch for one last chance at training him for racing.

Chapter 1

Raven's Son planted his feet, pulled against the rope around his neck, and refused to move forward. He reared and struck out at the three men who were trying to get him into the trailer. Watching the battle from the fence, Tom Blake shook his head. "Just leave him alone for a minute," he urged the others. "Look at him. He's terrified."

"He's not afraid," snarled one of the men. "He's just plain mean-spirited. He should be put down. He's no use for anything, and he's eventually going to hurt someone. It was just a matter of time before he killed one of us."

"He's not a killer," shouted Olivia, Tom Blake's daughter, who was perched on the fence next to her dad. "There's no such thing as a killer horse unless he feels threatened. Horses are prey animals, not predators. He's just obviously been mistreated and no longer trusts anyone on two legs," she asserted. "The way y'all are yelling and cursing at him, it's no wonder he's resisting."

"Are you saying I've mistreated this horse?" asked the stranger leaning against the gate of the paddock watching the others struggle. "I've trained lots of horses, young lady, and no one ever accused me of mistreating a single one of them. I agree with the others; this horse is a natural killer. He's mean through and through and should be put out of his misery."

Olivia was about to argue with the stranger when her Dad gave her the look she'd learn to recognize over the years as a warning that she needed to be quiet. She jumped down from the fence and shot a hateful glance at the stranger as she stormed off toward their truck. "I bet I could get that horse in the trailer, and I wouldn't need to be cursing and shouting at him either," she grumbled as she walked past him.

It was almost midnight when the three men finally forced Raven's Son into the trailer by locking arms behind his hindquarters and practically shoving him in headfirst. After the horse was loaded, Tom jumped into his truck and pulled away. Olivia was leaning up against the window with her face buried in a large pillow. She had her headset over her ears and pretended to be asleep.

A twinge of sadness ripped through Tom's heart as he realized Olivia was no longer his *little* girl. At twenty, she had blossomed into a real beauty, even though her choice of clothes and her lack of attention to her appearance hid her femininity. Jeans, flannel shirts, cowboy hats, and boots were the only clothes she owned and the only things she had ever worn.

Her mother abandoned them when Olivia was just an infant and left them alone to figure out how to rebuild their lives together. Shortly after deserting them, she died in an automobile crash. Since her death, Olivia's grandfather had made Tom's life a living hell—constantly stalking them and trying to take Olivia away from him in retaliation for the loss of his own daughter. So far, Tom had managed to keep Olivia away from her grandfather and from even knowing that he existed. Right or wrong, he had kept her from learning about her grandfather's selfish attempts to steal her away from him.

He shifted his weight in the seat of the truck and tried to shed the gnawing guilt he felt about depriving her of a life surrounded by the luxury that her grandfather could have provided her. He rationalized that all the luxuries in the world could never replace the love they had for one another and that she was much better off living in their meager state than being surrounded by wealth without love.

From the time she was born, Tom had been Olivia's protector. He was the one who took care of her and doctored her through all of her childhood diseases, cut her hair for her, and explained the onset of her womanhood. They had never been apart—not even for a day. He did the best he could by her, but he couldn't help but feel he missed the mark in helping her become the beautiful, young woman he knew she could become.

They led a transitory life following the rodeo circuit and never staying in one spot for more than a few weeks at a time, always keeping one step ahead of her grandfather and his army of detectives. Although she never complained about their constant moving, he felt guilty she never had a chance to develop friends with people her own age even though he had made sure she kept up with her education through home schooling and online instruction. Last year, she even completed an online associate's degree in Equine Science, but she never had a real date, never went out with a group of peers, never went to a prom, nor experienced any of the things other kids her age did. Her friends were old, worn out cowboys who loved her dearly and taught her things she could never learn from textbooks about nature and life, but none of them had shown her how to become a woman.

She was a skilled horsewoman, though. She could ride the wildest horses at the rodeo and run the barrels better than most of the men who competed against her. And somewhere along the way, she had learned to be a terrific cook, though her culinary skills were limited to hundreds of ways to make hamburger casseroles, pancakes, omelets, and biscuit baking. He was proud of Olivia and knew she deserved more than he had been able to give her.

He silently prayed this was his chance to make it up to her. Unexpectedly, Brett Kendall, a former high school friend, asked him to come to his ranch to train Raven's Son for Quarter Horse racing. Several other well-known trainers had already tried to work with the horse but had obviously failed. He glanced through the rear view mirror at his rusty, old horse trailer and hoped it would hold together until he got to the Kendall Ranch. It was a long drive from Whitesboro, Texas to Fredericksburg in Texas Hill Country. It would be morning before they got there, and he obviously couldn't stop as long as he was hauling a horse as belligerent as Raven's Son. He gripped the steering wheel tightly as the truck swayed from the constant shifting of weight of the distraught horse.

"This is going to be a long night," he muttered. He reached over, picked up one of Olivia's CDs, and slid it into the player. The soft, mellow voice of Jan Taylor, Olivia's idol and Brett Kendall's wife, filled the vacuum of silence in their old truck.

Chapter 2

Jan rolled over in the giant king-size bed and reached out for Brett. Without opening her eyes, she groped among the pillows but couldn't find him. Finally, she forced her eyes to open and tried to find him in the darkness. Unable to see anything, she rolled back over to her side of the bed and squinted to make out the shining red numbers on the digital clock. "Eight o'clock," she screeched as she jumped out of bed. "Half of the morning is gone, for heaven's sake."

She grabbed her robe and pushed the button on the nightstand to raise the room darkening shades. The Texas sun flooded the room with a blinding light and reminded her of the bright stage lights she hated because they screened out most of the audience during her concerts. "Brett," she called out as she hurried out of the bedroom.

"Good morning, sleepy head," said Brett as he offered her a large glass of fresh pineapple juice. "Pineapple juice for the woman with the golden voice." He smiled and kissed her lightly on the forehead.

Jan sipped the fresh pineapple juice. "Why did you let me sleep so long?" she moaned. "I promised Roger I'd be at the studio by ten, and I intended to help Justin with some of the new foals this morning. He's going to be furious with me."

"No, he won't," answered Brett as he pulled her into his arms. "I called your handsome nephew this morning and told him I was giving you the morning off. He was actually

18

glad because he wanted to go to the feed store early to get some of the new alfalfa coming in. See, I always have your back, Mrs. Kendall."

Jan reached up and wrapped her arms around his neck. "You're my knight in shining armor, Mr. Kendall." She kissed him softly on the lips and then drew in a deep breath. "Something sure smells good. Did you fix breakfast too?"

"I did," replied Brett. "I would have brought it to you in bed if you had just waited a minute." Brett winked at her and smiled broadly.

She stared up at his smiling face. Then, linking her fingers behind his neck, she kissed him again. He responded to her kiss by holding her so tightly she could barely breathe. "How much time do you have before you leave for the studio?" he whispered softly in her hair.

Jan laughed. "Sorry, big fellow, just long enough to eat some of that beautiful fruit plate and French toast before getting dressed and heading into town." She winked at him as she slid into the soft leather seat in the breakfast nook. "This looks delightful," she said. She grabbed her fork and pulled one of the Texas-sized pieces of French toast onto her plate. "What's on your schedule, today?" she asked.

"Don't tell me that you've forgotten?"

"Oh my gosh, I did forget. Raven's Son is due here today. I'm sorry. What time will he get here?" She had just gotten the words out of her mouth when the rattling sound of a beat up, old horse trailer and rust-laden pickup rumbled into the drive.

"Right about now," answered Brett. "Sorry, honey, gotta go." He jumped up from the table and gently kissed her on top of her head as he rushed out the back door.

Jan could hear the constant thuds against the back of the trailer as the horse inside seemed determined to knock down the rear door. A piercing, high-pitched whinny from inside the tattered trailer shattered the quiet morning. The same shrill whinny was immediately echoed from the breeding barn. "Like father, like son," she muttered. She quickly jumped up from the table, grabbed her jean jacket hanging on the knob by the back door, and shoved her bare feet into her boots as she rushed outside in her nightgown. She was still munching on the French toast she held in her hand as she reached the trailer.

"Honey, you'll catch cold out here dressed like that," warned Brett.

"I can't wait to see him, Brett."

Jan had never seen Raven's Son. He was foaled on a ranch north of Dallas near Whitesboro, Texas. Raven had sired many foals during the past four years but most were born at locations far from their ranch. She had seen several of them at horse shows, and, before their accident, she had even competed against some of them with Raven, who always beat all competitors, even his own offspring.

"Howdy, Tom," called Brett to the man coming around the front of his truck. "You must be exhausted after driving all night."

Jan smiled at Tom Blake and reached out to shake his hand. "Howdy, Tom, I'm Jan. Welcome to the Kendall Ranch."

"It's sure a pleasure to meet you, Mrs. Kendall," said Tom awkwardly wiping his hand off on his jeans before offering it to Jan. "I listened to your CDs all the way 'cross Texas last night. My daughter Olivia loves to hear you sing." Tom motioned toward the truck where Jan could see a young girl still asleep in the front seat with a pillow propped up against the window and a pair of headphones draped over her ears.

"Thank you. I'm flattered." Jan smiled and grabbed hold of Brett's arm. She tried not to stare at Tom, but his disheveled, rough appearance surprised her. Brett had told her that he and Tom had grown up together, but Tom looked much older than Brett. Deep creases in his tanned face, his stooped shoulders, and the lack-luster look in his eyes made him look considerably older.

She knew Tom once was one of the most respected trainers in Quarter Horse racing, until one of the fillies he trained for the All American Futurity had to be put down when her right front leg shattered as she charged from the starting gate. The autopsy and toxicology study on the horse indicated high levels of pain masking drugs, and Tom was accused of doping the animal to conceal the fact the horse was injured and should never have raced. Though Tom maintained his innocence in the whole affair, no one would hire him after that, not even to clean stalls.

To earn enough money to support Olivia, Brett told her Tom followed the rodeo circuit across the country. After all of the other well-known trainers refused to continue to train Raven's Son, Brett tracked him down in Oklahoma and talked him into coming to the ranch to train the colt. For the sake of both Tom and Brett, Jan hoped Tom could tame the wild beast now threatening to tear the worn out trailer apart.

As Brett was explaining to Tom which barn was assigned to Raven's Son, Jan walked to the back of the trailer. She began to whistle softly to the unruly animal. For a brief moment, Raven's Son stopped kicking against the trailer, but the moment she quit whistling, he immediately began again to pound his hooves against the rear door.

"I wouldn't get too close, Mrs. Kendall," called Tom. "I wouldn't trust that rear door to hold much longer."

"He sure is out of sorts," said Jan shaking her head. "Such a shame; I wonder who's to blame for causing all that anger?"

"I know several of the trainers who had him before," said Tom. "Their methods of breaking a horse are a lot different from mine. I imagine Sonny is so angry right now that it's going to take some sort of a miracle to calm him down."

"Sonny?" asked Jan. "Is that what they call him?"

"Olivia started calling him that last night," answered Tom. "I hope you don't mind. Raven's Son is such a mouthful to say."

"No, I like it," replied Jan. "It has a gentle sound to it, but I have to admit that right now the name doesn't seem to fit the angry horse." She frowned and turned away from the trailer to look directly at Tom. "You probably know his sire is over in our breeding barn. We moved Raven over here from my family's ranch when Brett and I were married. That was his whinny you heard answering Sonny's. He was quite a handful at first too, but my persistence won out in the end. Of course, he didn't have anyone but me messing with his mind. I sure hope you can undo what has been done to Sonny to make him so angry and obviously mistrusting."

"I sure intend to try, ma'am. I can't tell you how much I appreciate the chance y'all are giving me. I promise I'll give it everything I've got."

Jan was overwhelmed by the sadness in Tom's eyes. "We're the ones who are appreciative. You're taking on a huge task. Believe me; I know the wild blood that pumps through those veins," she said tossing her head toward Sonny. "I hope you'll let me help to win him over."

"Sure. I'll need all the help I can get. I saw you and Raven in the reining competition at the World Show several years back. You two were like watching a ballet of perfection. I know your skills with horses, and I hope you won't hesitate to help out whenever you can."

"Thanks, Tom. I don't know too much about racing, but I do know how to instill trust in horses. I think they sense how much I love and respect them. At least, I know Raven feels my love and respect, and he trusts me because of it."

"She's right, Tom," interrupted Brett. "Raven completely trusts her and no one else. He only tolerates me because of her. I still think he'd just as soon mow me down as to look at me, and he probably would if he didn't think it would upset Jan. That's why I stay on her good side," he said as he reached out and pulled Jan close to him and hugged her tightly around the waist.

"I wish I could hang around," said Jan, "but duty calls. I have a recording session in an hour, so I'd better get a move on. Welcome again, Tom."

Brett kissed her on the cheek, "Love ya, honey. Be careful driving to the studio, and don't let Roger keep you there all day." He leaned over and softly whispered in her ear, "We've got some unfinished business tonight after your walk with Raven."

Jan could feel herself blush as she quickly turned and walked into the house.

Chapter 3

Tom followed Brett's four-wheeler down a dirt road leading to the east side of the fifteen hundred acre Kendall Ranch. In the distance, he could see a two-story log cabin and a sturdy rock barn with a large, fenced paddock across the back. Next to the paddock, he spotted a round exercise pen and a mechanical walker. Behind the barn, he could make out a tract of land that had obviously been leveled to make a short racetrack. "Wow," he said. "This is perfect." He reached over and nudged Olivia. "Wake up, sweetie," he said. "We're in paradise."

Olivia stretched and moaned and then immediately snuggled back into the pillow. Tom gently lifted off the headset covering her ears. "Wake up, Olivia. I'm going to need your help unloading Sonny."

Olivia pulled her face out of the pillow and tried to focus her half-closed eyes. "Where are we?" she mumbled as she glanced through the window at the mesquite and rock covered land around her.

"We're at the Kendall Ranch," responded Tom. He glanced over at his daughter and watched her as she pulled the rubber band out of her hair and ran her fingers through the thick, blonde curls trying to smooth them back before replacing the ugly, red rubber band around them once again. She always wore her hair pulled away from her face in a long ponytail. No bows or fancy hair ties had ever been used to hold back her tangled, unruly curls. Once again, Tom felt the nagging disappointment of not providing her the chance to learn how to be a young lady.

"Wow, is that a real log cabin?" asked Olivia excitedly. "Is that where we'll stay, or is there an apartment for us in the barn?"

"I think the cabin is to be ours," answered Tom. "At least while we're here," he reminded her. He watched Olivia's body slump as she realized that, once again, this would be a temporary home.

"Well, at least it's a real house, and it's ours for now," she replied, quickly rebounding as she always did. Rolling down the window and sticking her head out to get a better look, she carefully surveyed the log and rock cottage. "I bet it's the original home of the first settlers on the ranch. I read an article on the Internet about the Kendall Ranch and found out it was first inhabited after the Civil War by a man and his family who migrated from Kentucky to Texas in 1865. Wow, we're going to live in a cottage full of history," she said with excitement. "What a treat."

Tom smiled at Olivia's enthusiasm. He wished he could tell her this was to be home forever, but he couldn't. At least being close to Jan Taylor-Kendall and living in the historic cabin would give her some joy, even if just for a while. "By the way," he said, "you missed the chance to meet Jan Taylor."

"You're joking, right? I know you wouldn't have let me miss meeting her. Surely, you didn't let me sleep through that chance." She turned around in the seat and glared at him.

"I did—sorry about that. She's a real knock out even in

a cotton night gown with boots and a jeans jacket. She came out to get a look at the horse. She seems real—no pretentiousness about her at all," replied Tom.

"I can't believe you didn't wake me," moaned Olivia.

"Don't worry, sweetie. I'm sure she'll be around. She offered to help us work with that menacing beast we've been hauling all night."

"She can work wonders with horses," Olivia replied excitedly. "I've read a lot about her in some of the horse magazines. Remember when we saw her a couple of years ago in Oklahoma? She and her stud Raven were amazing. I'll never forget watching them. They were like one body going through the reining pattern with wings."

Tom smiled at his daughter's admiration of her idol. "Well, now you'll have a chance to get that autograph you've been wanting to get," he replied. "But first, we have to manage to get that horse into the barn without anyone getting hurt. Are you ready?"

"Ready," said Olivia, bouncing out of the truck as Tom coasted to a stop. "Howdy," she called to Brett.

Brett smiled at the spunky, young blonde offering to shake his hand. "Welcome," he said. "You must be Olivia. I'm Brett Kendall."

"Nice to meet you, Mr. Kendall. I appreciate the chance you're giving to my dad. I know he won't disappoint you. He's the best horse trainer in the country," she announced.

"Cut the hype, Olivia," said Tom. "Brett and I grew up together, so he knows all about me."

"I'm sure you're right, Olivia," Brett replied, "but I'm afraid I may have given him a colossal challenge based on the noises coming from that trailer. I think we'd better get Sonny out of there before he tears it apart and ruins his feet and legs by beating them against that door."

"Right," said Tom. "Olivia, go open the gate to the paddock. I'm going to back the truck right inside of it, so when he bolts out of the trailer, he'll already be inside of the fence." Olivia took off at a sprint toward the gate.

"Is she always that full of energy?" remarked Brett.

"She's a spitfire, all right. She's got more spunk and grit than any of the young, wannabe cowboys that come out to the rodeos," called Tom as he climbed back into the truck. Brett watched as Tom skillfully swung the truck around and backed the trailer straight through the gate into the small paddock on the first try.

"Okay, Olivia. Get out of there, so I can let this monster out," called Tom heading to the back of the trailer. "We don't have a butt strap on him, so he's going to shoot out of here like a rocket."

"Got it, Dad. Watch yourself," warned Olivia.

Once he was assured Olivia was on the fence and out of harm's way, Tom pulled back the latches on the back door of the trailer. Sonny shot out of it so fast that the door swung around and slammed Tom against the trailer, knocking him to the ground.

Olivia jumped down from the fence, grabbed her dad by the collar of his shirt, and tried desperately to pull him across the paddock toward the gate. Brett quickly ran into the paddock, waving his hands to distract Sonny from Olivia and Tom.

Sonny reared and pawed the air, snorting and whistling wildly. He charged toward the trailer and then suddenly whirled around and galloped across the paddock leaving behind a cloud of dust. Brett rushed to help Olivia pull Tom through the gate and off to the side. A huge gash above Tom's left eye was bleeding profusely, and he was obviously dazed.

"We've got to get the gate closed before that crazy horse discovers he can squeeze past the trailer and get out," Brett yelled to Olivia. "As soon as I pull the truck out of the paddock, you're going to have to shut the gate as fast as you can."

"Got it," yelled Olivia. "Hang in there, Dad," she muttered as she clamored up from the ground.

Staying as close to the truck as possible, Brett kept his eyes on Sonny. When he opened the squeaky door of the truck, Sonny whirled around and began wildly running back and forth at the back of the paddock. Brett stomped on the gas and peeled through the gate with the rear doors of the rickety trailer swinging wildly.

Olivia looked up to see Sonny running toward her at breakneck speed as she tried desperately to close the huge, metal gate. Moving as quickly as she could, she managed to swing it shut, but she didn't have time to secure it before he reached it. Hoping to hold off his charge, she quickly turned around, buried her heels in the dirt, and pushed back with all her strength against the gate. Sonny slammed into it, sending her sprawling face first into the ground, and she quickly rolled to the side to avoid being trampled by him as he dashed out of the paddock.

Justin Livingston observed the chaos as he rode toward the paddock. Automatically, he uncoiled the lariat from his saddle horn and whirled it above his head. As Sonny sped past him, Justin threw the rope. It hit its target, encircling the speeding horse around his neck. Justin quickly spun his horse around, chasing after Sonny and keeping slack in the rope to avoid a dangerous jerk to Sonny's neck.

Unexpectedly, the frightened horse circled back and headed inside the paddock. Once inside the fenced area, Justin began slowly tightening the rope around the horn of his saddle as he tried to restrict Sonny's wild race around the corral. Finally, he brought his horse to a sliding stop and quickly made him back as he steadily continued to wrap more of the lariat around the horn of his saddle, slowly pulling Sonny toward him. The panicked horse reared and stuck out at Justin and his horse. "Whoa," yelled Justin. "No one is going to hurt you. Easy fellow," he called to Sonny.

Sonny continued to paw the ground, blowing and snorting menacingly. Justin quickly took out a knife and cut the rope connecting the two animals, making sure the end of the rope left around Sonny was short enough not to reach his feet and possibly trip him. He calmly started to back his horse toward the gate. Sonny made no attempt to charge the other horse but reared and struck out wildly.

"Be ready to secure the gate once I clear it," Justin calmly called to the others.

"We've got it," yelled Brett. Justin spun his horse around and sped through the gate. Olivia quickly slammed it shut again, and Brett managed to throw the latch chain across the gate post temporarily securing it, so another charge from Sonny wouldn't open it. Sonny reared high into the air striking out madly. When he lowered himself to the ground, he began racing frantically around the paddock whinnying and kicking his hind legs with such force he could barely be seen amidst the cloud of dust he whipped through the air.

"Good god, Olivia, are you okay?" yelled Tom who had managed to prop himself up against a fence post. He was squeezing his left leg tightly above the knee and holding a dirty handkerchief against the gash on his forehead.

"I'm fine," thundered Olivia. "I reckon that poor, little horse is as mad and as scared as I am." She attempted to brush the dirt from her clothes as she rushed over to where her dad was sitting.

"Poor little horse?" snarled Justin. "That crazy horse could have hurt all of us," he shouted.

"It's humans who've made him angry like that. It's not his fault he's the way he is," called Olivia over her shoulder as she reached her dad. "Here, let me take a look at your head." She leaned over and gently removed the dirty handkerchief. "Ooh, that's a nasty cut. That's going to require some stitching. Let's get you up and over to the house, so I can clean off the dirt and put in a couple of stitches."

As she was struggling to get her dad up from the ground, Justin rushed to help her. "Here let me help you," he offered.

"I can get him up by myself, if you don't mind," said Olivia.

"Whoa, sorry," said Justin. "I didn't mean to interfere." He shot her a disgusted look and started to walk away.

"Move over, Olivia," ordered Brett. "Come on back here, Justin. We need to carry him over to the house. The gash over his eye is not his only injury," he said and pointed to the blood seeping through Tom's jeans below his left knee.

"I'm okay," insisted Tom. "Those darn latches on the trailer door got me on the head and on my shin."

"Well, just in case there's something broken in that leg, I still think we should carry you over to the house," insisted Brett. "Come on, Justin, lock hold of my wrists under his knees and across his back. On three, lift him."

Justin brushed Olivia aside and knelt down to grab hold of Brett's wrists beneath Tom's legs. "Okay, I'm ready," he called to Brett.

"One, two, three, lift," shouted Brett.

Tom winced as the two men lifted him and headed toward the house. Olivia fell in behind them still smarting from their dismissal of her in helping her dad. She had been taking care of him her whole life. He was always getting hurt riding bulls in the rodeo. She had mended broken bones, deep wounds, and all sorts of torn ligaments and sore muscles. She certainly knew more than either of them about how to help her dad.

Inside the house, Brett and Justin lowered Tom slowly on to a straight back chair. Tom grabbed hold of his left knee and swallowed the urge to cry out when they put him down. Olivia pushed forward and whipped out a knife from her pocket. She skillfully slit open Tom's jeans neatly following the seam line, so they could easily be re-stitched. Gently pulling open the leg of his pants, she stared at the bone visible through the deep gash on his left shin. "Wow, Dad. That's cut clear to the bone. I think this one is going to have to be taken care of by a real doctor."

A loud thud behind them attracted their attention to where Justin had been standing. He was sprawled out on his back on the thick braided rug that covered the wooden plank floor and had obviously fainted at the sight of Tom's wound.

Olivia burst out laughing. "Now that's a real cowboy," she remarked unsympathetically.

"Show a little compassion, Olivia," groaned Tom. "Not everyone handles this type of thing like you do. Help Brett revive the poor guy, for Pete's sake."

"What happened?" moaned Justin as Brett wiped his face with a cold cloth.

"You fainted, strong man," said Olivia sarcastically. "I bet this isn't the first time you've conked out at the sight of bones and blood, is it?"

Justin sat up and slapped his hat back on his head. "I've never fainted in my life," he stormed. "I tripped over the rug and fell backward. That's all."

Trying to keep a straight face, Brett reached out to help Justin up from the floor.

"Yeah, I bet," responded Olivia chuckling. "Who are you anyway?" she asked.

"This is my wife's nephew," replied Brett. "Justin Livingston, meet Olivia Blake, Tom's daughter."

"Hmm," mocked Olivia. "You obviously don't take after your fabulous aunt."

Justin just stared at Olivia and frantically searched for a searing remark but nothing came to mind. Finally deciding to ignore her, he turned around to Brett, "Do you want me to call for the helicopter lift, or are you going to take him into town in your truck?"

"Don't bother with the helicopter, Brett," said Tom quickly. "Olivia can take me into town in our truck. Just give us directions. We've already caused enough trouble for you.

And don't worry about this slowing me down. I'll be able to start working with Sonny the first thing tomorrow. A couple of stitches and a sturdy cast and I'll be good to go."

Brett stared down at Tom's pleading eyes. He suspected that Tom probably was worrying about the medical expenses and fearful that Brett would decide to bring someone else in to train the horse. "Whatever you want to do, Tom. I'll just call ahead and let the hospital know you're on your way. They've got a dynamite orthopedic doctor there, so I'll make sure he sees you as soon as you arrive. And by the way, my insurance will cover this, so don't pay the bill when you leave."

Tom heaved a long, deep sigh as Brett reached over and gently took hold of his shoulder. "Hang in there, Buddy," he said. Brett then turned to Justin and motioned for him to leave.

"Don't you think we should load him into the truck?" asked Justin. "How will she be able to get him in by herself?"

"Don't you worry your weak stomach about that," said Olivia. "I have this covered."

Tom shot a look of disgust at his mouthy, young daughter. "Thanks for your help, Justin. Things could have gotten pretty ugly out there if you hadn't shown up and taken control of the situation like you did. We really appreciate your help."

Olivia took her cue from her dad's sharp glance. "Yeah, thanks," she muttered.

Chapter 4

It was almost dark when Olivia pulled the truck into the driveway that led back to the historical log cabin they would call home for a while. She intentionally drove slowly down the dusty road to avoid jostling her dad, who was resting in the bed of the truck on an air mattress they slept on whenever they drove across country between rodeos. He was still drowsy from the medication they gave him at the hospital, and she contemplated letting him just sleep in the truck until morning. She knew the truck's camper shell would keep him warm and dry through the night.

When she finally reached the cabin, she turned off the noisy rumbling of the truck's engine and reached behind her to slide open the back window so she could see if her dad was still sleeping. Satisfied that he was resting comfortably, she reached through the window and placed his cell phone on the pillow beside his head and tucked hers into her jeans pocket. She also checked to make sure his well-used crutches were within his reach, even though she was confident that he would probably sleep through the night without stirring.

Climbing out of the truck, she slowly mounted the four wooden steps to the house. The boxes she had quickly unloaded earlier from the back of the truck were still stacked on the porch. She decided she would deal with them in the morning. Right now she was looking forward to a warm shower. When she opened the door, the smell of beef stew filled the air. Flipping on the light, she saw a bouquet of blue bonnet wildflowers on the table and an envelope laying next to it. On the kitchen counter, there was a large crockpot and a freshly baked pie. She tore open the envelope and took out the handwritten note inside.

Dear Tom and Olivia,

I am sorry your welcome to our ranch wasn't a pleasant one. Hopefully, the beef stew and pie will help bring you some comfort. I took the liberty of stocking the pantry and refrigerator with a few staples until you can shop for what you want. Please don't hesitate to call us at the main house if you need anything. I wrote the number on the chalkboard by the phone.

I hope you don't mind that I let myself into the cabin, but I wanted to keep the stew warm for your return and to put the groceries away. I also fed Sonny and left behind a babysitter.

Sincerely,
Jan

"A baby sitter? What in the heck does that mean?" Olivia wondered. She stared in disbelief at the handwritten note. She couldn't believe Jan Taylor had actually written a personal note to her and her dad. She clutched the note to her chest and squealed with delight.

For the first time in a long while, she felt as if things were going to be all right for her and her dad, in spite of their rocky start. Her dad was a quick healer, and she knew he wouldn't let an injured leg slow him down. She heaved a long sigh of relief as she began to explore the cozy cabin.

The first floor was completely open with a large, combined kitchen, eating, and living area. Across the front of the room, two large windows overlooked the long porch where four rocking chairs and a porch swing at one end suggested a quiet place to unwind after a long day's work. In the living room, there was a massive, rock fireplace surrounded by a large, leather sofa and two comfortable-looking, leather recliners. A beautiful, hand-braided rug stretched across the wooden-plank floors in front of the fireplace. On top of the rug sat a unique, glass-top coffee table resting on a pedestal made from a large rack of antlers. Next to the fireplace was a well-preserved, double-door antique cabinet with a butterfly motif beautifully hand-painted on the doors. On top of the cabinet was a modern flat-screened TV. "A nice blend of contemporary and antiques," she said. "Someone has exceptional taste and a flair for decorating—probably Jan Taylor."

Behind the recliners, a massive, antique desk stood in the center of the long wall. Olivia ran her hands carefully along the ridges of its large roll-top. She was startled at the instant, automatic retraction of the top as she pulled out the writing surface and exposed a row of neatly divided compartments and small drawers inside. "It's like the desk I saw in the museum in Philadelphia. I bet these pieces were the original furniture of the founders of the ranch," she said with a smile.

At the opposite end of the room was a modernized kitchen with a huge, round oak-table in the center of the eating area. Antique Windsor chairs provided seating for at least six around the refurbished table. "Oh, how I hope to have the chance to fix a meal for the Kendalls some evening," she muttered. "I bet they would like my biscuits." She lifted the lid on the crockpot that Jan had left and stared at the huge chunks of roast beef suspended in rich gravy and surrounded by large pieces of potatoes, onions, and carrots. She inhaled a long, deep breath. "Oh my gosh," she muttered, "it smells amazing."

Carefully placing the lid back on the crockpot, she headed toward a doorway off the main living area that led to a bedroom with an attached bathroom that had been modernized with a shower and Jacuzzi. A small stone fireplace lined the outer wall of the bedroom, and adjacent to it was a large window overlooking the barn and paddock area. "This will be dad's room. He'll need to be on the first floor, especially now," she decided. "Okay, next—where to find the stairs leading to the upper level?" she said as she returned to the living area.

She quickly spotted the narrow stairway off the kitchen. At the top of the stairs, a short hallway led to a single bedroom. It was a large, open room with slanted ceilings. There were two, huge dormer windows with built-in window seats overlooking the front of the house and a smaller, side window that provided a view of the barn and paddock. An antique writing desk and small, wooden chair were placed under the side window. In addition to the writing desk, the bedroom was furnished with a queen-size, four-poster bed, an antique armoire, and two chests. Shelves next to the armoire were no doubt intended for shoes (of which she had none), but they would certainly hold her one pair of boots and her cherished books and CDs.

A beautiful, white quilt with a large star pattern of soft pink, blue, and green in the center covered the bed. She recognized the quilt pattern as the Broken Star. The one craft she loved was the making of quilts. She had made and sold dozens of them over the years, but she had never tackled the difficult Broken Star pattern because the tiny size of the pieces in the giant pattern intimidated her.

Lace curtains added an additional bit of daintiness and femininity to the room. "All this fussiness is certainly wasted on me," she said as she stared at herself in the free-standing, full-length mirror. "Oh my gosh," she moaned and leaned closer to the mirror. "My face still has dirt streaks all over it from my fall when that crazy horse sent me sprawling head first, and my hair is filthy with grit and dust. I obviously have made an interesting first impression on everyone I've met today, but at least Jan Taylor didn't see me looking like this," she consoled herself.

She leaned across the desk and peered through the window, trying to see if Sonny was still running around in the paddock. To her surprise, she saw no movement in the paddock at all, but she did notice a small light glowing inside of the barn. "Hmm," she said. "I guess I'll have to go check on him, but not until I've had a warm bath and a bowl of that delicious smelling stew."

A small alcove off to the left of her bedroom housed a second bathroom. She gazed admiringly at the old claw-foot tub with a hand-held shower. Above the small stand-alone sink hung a mirror encased in a beautiful, antique brass frame. A narrow chest next to the tub was full of thick, fluffy towels and some toiletries. "Perfect," she said, smiling broadly and heaving a deep sigh of satisfaction.

She returned to the porch to get her box of clothes and to check on her dad. Satisfied that he was still resting peacefully in the truck, she picked up the box and lugged it up the narrow stairs to her room. Feeling exhausted from the day's events, she turned on the antique faucet above the tub and began to fill it with warm water. Spotting some bath salts in the cabinet, she sprinkled some under the stream of water, and the room was instantly filled with the pleasant scent of lilacs. "Ahh, this is the life," she muttered as she slid into the bubbles and drew in a deep breath, filling her lungs with their fragrance. "I could get used to this."

It had been a long, fretful day, but peace finally arrived with the sunset. She gazed out of the small, round window above the tub at the beautiful, orange evening sky. In the distance, she could hear the shrill whinny of a horse. *That must be Raven. I read about how he and Jan take a walk every night as the sun sinks below the horizon.* She sighed and wondered if she would ever have a daily routine in her own life. "I hope so, someday," she said as she ducked beneath the bubbles and felt the dirt of the day simply melt away.

Chapter 5

Jan quietly slipped out of the house without waking Brett and headed for the barn. It was just daybreak, and she wanted to spend some time with Sonny before she headed over to the Triple Bar Ranch to help Justin with the cow horse training. She stopped at the breeding barn to feed Raven and then headed for the main barn. She quickly bridled her new chestnut mare and put a halter and lead rope on Bud, her faithful, ten year-old gelding.

When she got near the cabin, she was relieved to see that Sonny wasn't racing around in the paddock. Her babysitter scheme must have calmed him down at least a little. There were no lights on in the cabin, and she realized the Blakes must have been exhausted after their ordeal yesterday, so they would probably sleep in a little today. Of course, she didn't actually know much about their work schedule, but under normal circumstances, she felt certain Tom would be up by now. He surely knew about the soaring Texas heat and humidity during the day and would naturally want to do his training before sunrise.

She tied the horses to the rail of the fence and headed into the barn. When Tom stepped out of the shadows and greeted her, she jumped and gasped.

"Sorry," he muttered. "I didn't mean to frighten you."

"Oh my gosh, I didn't expect to see you since there were no lights on in the house."

"The meds they gave me at the hospital knocked me out, so

Olivia just let me sleep all night in the truck. I know she's probably exhausted, so I didn't want to wake her with the clumping of crutches on those wooden steps. I was sure grateful to find the crock-pot, pie, and coffee pot in the barn with your note. Thanks. The stew and pie were delicious."

"Actually I left everything but the coffee pot in the house. Olivia must have carried the crockpot and pie out here last night. She probably suspected you'd come out here rather than go into the house."

Tom smiled. "She's a great kid. Well, not so much of a kid anymore," he corrected. "She knows me well, though; that's sure the truth. She's also great around the horses. She's a dynamite barrel racer and can ride just about any horse."

Although she had not met Olivia, Jan knew she liked her. *Anyone that considerate of her dad and who loved horses has to be worth knowing,* she decided. "How are you feeling?" she asked, noticing that Tom's eye was swollen completely shut.

"I don't feel as bad as I look," he muttered.

"Please, don't feel you have to push yourself, Tom. You really should give yourself a week or so to heal before you start working with Sonny."

"Nah. I'm fine really," he answered. He grabbed his crutches and headed toward Sonny's stall.

Jan sensed he didn't want any more sympathy or suggestions

that he should take it easy. "Looks like Nanny did the trick," she said peering into the stall.

Sonny was snuggled comfortably up to the old goat that Jan had brought over yesterday afternoon.

"She certainly did. Horses sure hate to be alone," replied Tom. "I appreciate the old goat. Her presence has certainly helped calm down that poor, angry colt. Now if we can just get him to trust us. I'm afraid that won't be as easy."

"You're right. It won't be as simple, but I've brought along some carrots and a stick to start the process."

"Yeah?" said Tom.

"My stick is tied to the fence out there, and I have a slew of different kinds of carrots."

Tom hobbled over to the door of the barn and saw Bud tied to the fence. "Aha," he said. "So you intend to teach Sonny that he's not the only boss around, right?"

"Right. It won't take Bud long to show him who's the boss. I think the pecking order among horses helps to start the dismissive process that can eventually lead to yielding respect to the trainer, don't you think so?"

"It's certainly worth a try," agreed Tom.

"Okay. Then I'm going to turn Bud loose in the paddock, unless you want to wait until Olivia wakes up. The ruckus will probably be heard for miles."

"She sleeps with her headset on," explained Tom. "She listens to one of your CDs every night. She probably won't wake up, but she'll kill me if you leave before she gets a chance to meet you. She's a hard-core fan."

Jan laughed. "I would like to meet her. She sounds like someone I'd enjoy knowing."

"Well, believe me when I tell you that she knows the words to every song on every one of your CDs she owns. She doesn't listen to any other country music, just yours."

"I appreciate fans like her. They're the ones I look for at my concerts," said Jan. "But I can't stay around too long this morning because I have to ride over to my family's ranch to help my nephew Justin. I heard you had a chance to meet him yesterday."

"Thank goodness he appeared when he did, or we could have had a real mess on our hands. He was like the cavalry riding straight into the fray," said Tom.

"He's a great kid; well, like Olivia, he's not much of a kid anymore. He graduates this week from Texas A&M with a degree in Animal Husbandry. He'll eventually take over the ranch when my sister and her husband retire. Right now he's the head trainer of all of our horses." Jan looked down at her watch. "If you don't think it will wake Olivia, I'd better turn Bud loose now." She headed out of the barn and walked quickly over to where her horses were patiently waiting by the paddock.

Tom grabbed his crutches and followed her.

Jan quickly removed the halter and lead rope from Bud and sent him into the paddock just as Sonny came darting out of the barn with the old goat close behind. "Well, here goes," she shouted. She laughed as Nanny quickly retreated back inside the barn. Nanny had seen this battle before and knew she was safer inside the stall.

Sonny charged at Bud, and Bud reared and pawed the air, whinnying wildly. He then lowered himself to the ground and charged at Sonny with his ears flattened tightly against his head and his teeth bared. Sonny reared once again and then whirled around and began circling the paddock with Bud chasing right beside him lightly nipping at his side.

After several circles around the paddock, Sonny stopped, and Bud slowly approached him. He rested his massive head on Sonny's back just behind his withers. Sonny dropped his head, and the pecking order was established. He accepted his subordinate position and submitted to Bud as the dominant horse in the pecking order.

"Wow, that was quick," said Tom.

"Bud always makes it quite clear that he's the boss. Even Raven doesn't challenge him," said Jan.

A stream of light spread out over the paddock, and Jan glanced up at the cabin. For a brief moment, Olivia's face was pressed against the upstairs window, and then she quickly disappeared.

Tom laughed. "I bet she doesn't even take time to get dressed before she darts out here."

Within seconds, the front door of the cabin flew open, and a nightgown clad Olivia flew down the stairs carrying several of Jan's CDs in her hand. Jan was impressed with the natural beauty of the young woman running toward the paddock in her bare feet with blonde curls streaming behind her like a golden halo in the light of the early dawn.

"Good morning, Miss Taylor," Olivia called breathlessly. "I know y'all are busy out here, but before you leave, can you please sign my CDs?"

"I'll be glad to sign them, but I think you'd better go get some boots on before you step on one of these limestone rocks and cut yourself."

"Oh, my feet are as tough as nails," replied Olivia. "I just didn't want to take the chance of missing you again. I know you have a tour coming up, so you'll probably be leaving the ranch soon, and you might not be back before we leave," she babbled.

Jan reached out and took the CDs Olivia shoved toward her. "Right, I do have a tour coming up, but I'm hoping the training relationship with your dad will become a long-term partnership, so we'll have lots of opportunity to see one another and to become friends."

Tom dropped his head and wobbled a little on his crutches. Olivia quickly grabbed hold of him and looked up at him with her face beaming. Neither of them had missed Jan's suggestion of a longtime partnership and the possibility of a permanent home with a chance to develop real friendships.

Jan noticed their startled reaction to her suggestion of a long-term partnership and was deeply saddened by the realization that such a possibility probably hadn't been offered to them for a long time. *What a transient and difficult life they must have been living,* she thought. *Hopefully, Brett and I can bring some stability back into their lives.*

Tom cleared his throat and rubbed his eyes. He pulled a crumbled, blood stained handkerchief from his back pocket and blew his nose. "The dust those two horses stirred up is getting to me," he mumbled as he shoved the handkerchief back into his jeans pocket. "Well, Jan, I've seen your stick work, now what about your carrot?"

Jan looked down at her watch again. "I'm afraid I have to come back later for the carrot training. I've got to head over to the Triple Bar to help Justin," she said. "Olivia, I promise I'll sign your CDs later, if you don't mind." She handed the CDs back to Olivia and reached in her jeans pocket to pull out a bunch of peppermints and placed them in Tom's rough hand. "Here," she said, "these are part of my carrot program. Keep some in your pocket, and when and if Sonny gets near, offer him one. Raven loves them. You might also try some music with him. I always sing to Raven. I've found music soothes the souls of animals as well as humans."

She turned toward the paddock and whistled a shrill, piercing sound through her fingers that echoed through the valley. Bud immediately trotted to the gate as she climbed over the fence and dropped into the paddock.

"Ms. Kendall, I'm not sure you should get in there with Sonny loose," worried Tom.

"He won't bother me with Bud here," she said. "I just want to say goodbye to Bud and give him his orders."

Sonny paced back and forth at the other end of the paddock but made no attempt to come to the gate.

Jan reached up and pulled Bud's face close to her. "I gotta go," she whispered hugging him around the neck. "I'm counting on you to help out here. You know what has to be done." Bud softly nickered and rubbed his face up and down against her jacket.

Tom carefully opened the gate just wide enough to allow Jan out. She chuckled at his obvious nervousness. "Believe me, Tom. Sonny's not going to go anywhere Bud doesn't want him to go."

Nanny peeked her head around the stall door. "See you, Nanny," called Jan, and Nanny responded with a soft, friendly bleat.

"I swear," said Olivia. "You're like a Doctor Doolittle."

Jan laughed and easily hopped onto the big, chestnut mare. "I wish I *could* talk to them," she said. "It would sure make training and caring for them a lot easier. See you later," she called as she galloped across the field.

"Isn't she great," shrieked Olivia.

"Yeah," muttered Tom. "She's quite a lady. Hey, how about one of your amazing breakfasts? I haven't even had a tour of our new home."

"Breakfast comes after you shower and shave. You stink," called Olivia over her shoulder as she raced back to the house. She knew better than to offer to help her Dad climb the stairs. He was a master at doing anything on crutches. He had experienced more sprains, strains, and breaks than she could count on both hands. Besides, she had noticed he stood a little bit taller after Jan Taylor mentioned a long-term partnership, and she wouldn't do anything in the world that might take away any of that restored pride in himself. She hadn't seen his eyes shine like that in a long time, maybe never.

Chapter 6

It was almost seven o'clock when Jan rode into the large, covered outdoor arena at the Triple Bar. "Where have *you* been?" asked Justin disgustedly. "We agreed to start at six this morning. I had to round up the calves by myself."

"I know. I'm sorry. I stayed too long at the ranch with the Blakes. I took Bud over there to establish a pecking order with Sonny," Jan explained.

Justin rode up next to her and stared at her for a moment. "Well, just let me know if you've decided to take over the training of Raven's Son or whatever you want to call him. If you want to quit helping me get our own horses ready for this year's competition, you'd better tell me now." He whirled his horse around and sped to the gate to allow one of the calves into the arena.

"Hey, young man," yelled Jan spurring her horse and shooting across the arena after him. "What in the heck is your nose all bent out of shape about?" she asked sliding her mare to a quick stop.

"I don't know what you mean?" shouted Justin. "I just know we have a heck of a lot of horses to get into shape before the major competitions, and it would be reassuring if I could count on you to help. All I ask is, if you want to mess around with Raven's Son and the Blakes, have the decency to let me know, so I can figure out how I'm going to get all of our training done by myself."

Jan reached over and yanked on the reins of Justin's horse causing it to whirl around and almost dump him on the ground. "What is your real problem, Justin? Your attitude has nothing to do with me being late, does it?"

"I have no idea what you're talking about," Justin answered. He jerked his reins away from Jan and sped down the arena chasing the calf.

For the next several hours, they worked in silence, taking turns either doing the arena work with their competition horses or bathing down the horses they had already worked. Jan finally broke the silence. "I don't think this grey mare has any cow in her at all," she said. "We may as well forget about her for the Futurity. She might do all right in some derbies, but she's not Futurity material."

"Let me see you work with her before we make the final decision," responded Justin coolly.

Jan opened the gate to allow one of the cows into the arena. She let the cow wander around for a minute or so, trying to determine if the mare would automatically start tracking it. The grey was totally disinterested in the calf and made no attempt to follow its movements. She only responded to changes in the direction of the calf when Jan used the reins and her legs to force her to track it. "See what I mean. She has no natural cow sense at all," shouted Jan.

"Yeah, I see what you're talking about." Justin heaved a long, audible sigh. "I was hoping we could sell her to the Fletchers. They've been looking for a good cow horse for the Reno Futurity." He jumped down off the arena wall and grabbed hold of the bridle of the gray mare as Jan slipped out of the saddle. "Well, I can't sell her to them for that level of competition," he said. He looked over at Jan and then quickly reached out to give her a hug. "I'm sorry about this morning. I was out of line."

"I forgive you," responded Jan, lightly kissing him on the cheek. "Maybe your attitude had to do with your fall over at the Blakes," she teased.

"I didn't faint," Justin protested vehemently.

"I didn't say you fainted," responded Jan. "I said you fell, but I'm thinking it wasn't a rug that caused your fall. I'd bet the proceeds from my next tour that the reason for your fall was that young blonde over there."

Oh, no you don't," shouted Justin. "Don't go getting me mixed up in your little romantic schemes. She's arrogant, contentious, and a genuine tomboy. There's absolutely nothing feminine about her that would make me even consider giving her a second look."

Jan laughed. "Well, then, I guess you won't mind if I invite her and her dad to your graduation party this weekend."

"I'd rather you didn't," shouted Justin as Jan led the grey mare into the barn. "Anyway, I have a date for the party."

Jan grabbed the hose in the bathing stall and aimed it right at him. She laughed when he jumped sideways to avoid the wet spray.

53

"Stop it, Aunt Jan. You'll ruin my hat," he yelled.

"Sorry, I just couldn't resist. You looked like you were about to have a meltdown," she said. "Anyway, I didn't suggest that you invite her as your date, but the fact that you mentioned it means you must have thought about her as date potential."

"I never had any such thought, believe me," replied Justin, brushing off his hat. "Can we talk about something else? This conversation is ended, never to be brought up again," he said with authority.

"You wanna bet," teased Jan. She attached the ties to the halter of the grey mare and began to wash her down.

"Yes. I'm serious," he replied whirling around and glaring at his aunt. He walked over to the bench outside of the bathing stall and plopped down on it. "We need to stop talking silliness and focus on how we're going to get our horses ready for the point shows, so we can be eligible for this year's major competitions. You have a tour coming up, and you'll be gone off and on for at least six weeks," he reminded her.

He was right. Jan knew once the tour started she would be in and out of the ranch for at least six weeks. She sighed, regretting that even after all Roger had done to reduce the amount of time that she had to spend on the road, she was still struggling with balancing her singing career with her love for horses and arena competitions. "What about Jamie and Jim?" she asked hoping to find a solution to her own absence.

54

"Did you see either of them out here helping this morning?" asked Justin. "My dear sister is so wrapped up in planning her big wedding and completing her veterinary internship that she hasn't been out here riding for over a week, and you know that Jim and mom are overwhelmed with trying to figure out ways to survive the predicted drought with the cattle operation. Jim tries to help out at least a couple of mornings a week, but he has to take care of the daily operations of the ranch. We can't afford to lose our cattle business. It's our survival. So now, that leaves just me to do all the training and competing."

"Wow, Justin. I'm sorry. I guess I've sort of lost track of the big picture."

"You and everyone else around here," he pouted. "You, of all people, should know we make our money from competitions, breeding, and sales. I've already given up training nothing but our own stock," he said.

"Why? You're starting to build a reputation as a great trainer."

"The money I got from training outside horses was just even dollars," explained Justin. "By the time I paid for feed, hay, bedding, and other general maintenance, I barely broke even and often went in the hole. It just wasn't worth my time." He took his hat off and twirled it around on his finger, staring at it as if he were looking for an answer to his problem. "And now, with sale prices sliding downward and fewer competitors registering for the big shows, prize monies are also bound to go down. I'm not sure how much longer we can keep the horse operation going."

"But our breeding program is still doing well," reminded Jan.

"Right," agreed Justin, "but don't forget that our breeding income is directly tied to our success in the show ring. The more we win, the more our stud services and sales go up. That brings me back to the point that, if we don't keep our horses in shape, and we don't compete in the big shows, the whole horse program starts a downward spiral."

Jan turned off the water and neatly wrapped the hose around the reel attached to the wall to give herself time to think about what Justin had just said. She was deeply concerned about his suggestion of possibly ending the horse operation. Her family had bred, raised, and trained horses for generations, and she couldn't imagine not continuing to do so. "You're not really thinking of doing away with the horse operation, are you? You can't let that happen."

"That's not what I want; you know that. The horse operation is my life. It's all I've ever known or wanted to do. I'm just saying that I'm sort of between a rock and a hard spot here with both you and Jamie not helping out. I can't really afford to take on another full-time trainer; you know that."

For several minutes, both of them were quiet—lost in their own thoughts. Jan ran the curved scraper over the gray mare to help dry her off and then led her out of the bathing stall. She looked over at Justin and could see the concern in his young eyes. *It's not fair*, she thought. *He's too young to have so much on his shoulders. He loves ranching, and*

56

I don't know what will happen to him if the whole thing goes belly-up between the predicted drought and the tight economy. "Look, Justin, I have an idea, but I don't think you're going to like it at first but just hear me out, OK?"

"If you already know I'm not going to like it, why bother suggesting it?" he asked.

"All right, then I won't tell you," she called over her shoulder. She led the mare up and down the aisle several times to finish drying her off before putting her back into her stall. She simply waited without saying another word, knowing that Justin would eventually give in and ask her about her plan.

After several minutes, Justin once again lost the waiting game and called out, "C'mon, don't do this silent treatment thing to me. You know I hate it. It's just a ploy you use to make me hear you out. You do it all the time, and I can't help but get suckered in."

Jan laughed. "So, does that mean you will at least listen to my idea?"

"Do I really have any choice? You know you're eventually going to tell me anyway."

Jan closed the door to the mare's stall. She turned around to face Justin and leaned up against the door, drawing in a deep breath. "OK, here goes. You know Olivia Blake..."

"Stop," shouted Justin. "Don't go any further. I am not going to have Olivia Blake help me train horses, and that's final. She's a barrel racer for heaven's sake. What could she possibly know about reining and cow horse training."

"I wasn't going to suggest that she help with the training, although if she's as good a horsewoman as her dad says she is, she could probably learn to work with the horses on the basics."

"I'm not interested, so just forget it," argued Justin.

Jan walked down the aisle and put her arm across his shoulder. "Hey," she started, "you promised to hear me out."

"I've heard enough already," interrupted Justin. He shrugged his shoulders and tossed Jan's arm off. "I don't want her hanging around here, and that's final. Besides, I assume she'll be helping her dad with Raven's Son."

"True," said Jan, "but I would guess they will do their training before day break, and you could push your training up a little."

"What?" he shouted. "You want me to work our own horses during the heat of the day? That's real considerate of you." He turned and walked toward the barn door.

"Now, come on Justin. Don't put up false arguments. They won't be doing any real training with Sonny for a while. They have a lot of work to do just building a relationship with the horse right now. You saw how tormented he is. And besides, we both know by next month, we'll start working our horses between midnight and four in the morning to avoid the heat and humidity." She followed him out of the barn, running to catch up with him. When she finally reached him, she hooked her arm through his. "Look, at least she could bathe the horses after you've worked them and then saddle the next horse you'll be riding. Just think about how much time that would save you," she argued.

"Not interested," shouted Justin as he pulled away from her and jogged toward the house.

Chapter 7

Olivia wandered out onto the porch after cleaning up the kitchen from dinner. "Hey, Pop," she said. "How're you feeling?" She plopped down on the porch swing next to her dad and leaned over to kiss him gently on the cheek.

"I'm doing OK," responded Tom. "I was just thinking about *you*."

"Me?" asked Olivia. "What about?"

"Well," started Tom, "I was just wondering if you think you're gonna like it here?"

"Like it? I love it here," Olivia replied quickly. "The weather, the wide open range behind the barn, the majestic looking ridge in the distance—what's not to like?" she asked. "It's exactly the kind of place where I always dreamed of living."

"The ranch *is* beautiful," responded Tom thoughtfully, "but I was thinking more about the isolation. I love being out here away from the raging rat race, but what about you? You're still young. Are you sure you can handle the loneliness of living out here so far from other people and other things?"

"We're not that isolated. The Kendalls are nearby, and the Triple Bar ranch is close. We haven't met the other Livingstons yet, but we will."

"Yeah, I know, but I don't know if it's the right thing for you to be so limited in the people you'll have the chance to meet and to be so isolated from the things you might want to do. You should be exploring the world outside of rodeos and horse racing. How will you ever know if there's something you'd like better, if you've never had a chance to explore other ways of living?" Tom watched his daughter carefully.

"C'mon, Dad," said Olivia. "Have you forgotten we've traveled back and forth across this country a dozen times and have been in every major city from New York to L.A.? The rodeo circuit provided a lot of opportunity for me to see this country and to meet people from all over."

"True," Tom agreed, "but you never actually had the chance to live anywhere for more than a month or so, and the only people you've really met are old cowboys and young wannabes."

"I've met enough personality types and experienced enough big and small town living to know what I want out of life," said Olivia. "Don't you worry about me," she said draping her arm around her dad's shoulder. "I'm as happy as a lark out here."

Tom leaned over and gave his young daughter a quick kiss on the cheek. "You're something else, sweetie," he said.

"Yes, I am," agreed Olivia. "I just don't know exactly what that something is yet, but I do know this is exactly where I want to live. I can discover who I really am right here better than anyplace else on earth."

Tom patted his daughter on the shoulder. "You're young, and you can become whatever and whoever you want to be. I just don't want to be the reason you haven't had the chance to try out all of your options."

"Please, Dad, don't worry. I couldn't have asked for a better father. I love you," she said as she leaned her head against his strong shoulder.

For several minutes, they just sat there enjoying each other and the soft sounds of the night. As the sun slipped below the horizon, in the distance they heard the distinctive whinny of a horse as he bade farewell to another day. Olivia smiled. "There goes Raven."

"He's some horse," responded Tom. "If Sonny turns out to be half as athletic as Raven, we'll have a real winner on our hands for sure."

"Sonny's got greatness bred in him that's just dying to come out, only he's just a little confused right now," replied Olivia.

Tom smiled. "I hope you're right, about his greatness I mean."

"You didn't get to see how he tore across the paddock the other day. He covered that distance in nothing flat. One minute he was at the back fence, and within seconds, he was out that gate."

"He's certainly bred for speed. I just hope we can get him to trust us. He sure is angry at the world right now."

"You'll win him over, Dad. You'll see. I know you will."

Tom heaved a long, audible sigh. "I hope so, darlin'. I certainly hope so. This colt is my chance—maybe my last chance."

Olivia glanced up at her dad. The sadness in his eyes grabbed at her heart. She didn't know what to say. He was right. Sonny was perhaps his last chance to get his dignity back. *If dad can't get that colt to do what I know he can do, what will become of both of them,* she wondered. She knew her dad would never go back to the rodeo. He was way past his prime to compete any longer riding the broncos and the bulls. Horses and racing were his true passion. A sudden, deep sense of sadness swept through her.

"Pretty sunset," muttered Tom.

Olivia looked out beyond the pasture at the towering rocky ridge in the distance. She could still see just the tip of the massive round sun and a panorama of orange streaks across the sky. *Keep your eyes on heaven*, she muttered to herself recalling the words to her favorite Jan Taylor song. *Please, God,* she silently prayed. *Touch Sonny and heal his angry spirit. Make him understand, please.*

"Look," whispered Tom, pointing toward the paddock. Sonny had just wandered out of the barn and was walking toward the orange horizon. "Why don't we saunter out there to get him used to having us around? Do you have your harmonica? Maybe some melancholy music will soften his troubled, young heart."

Olivia quickly jumped up from the swing and handed the crutches to her dad. "I'll go and get it," she said as she darted into the house. "Meet you out there," she called.

Tom smiled as he watched her race up the stairs to her room. *Oh, to be that young and that full of life and hope*, he mused as he hobbled down the steps.

Olivia was back in a flash and ran past him on the path to the barn. "I'll get you the lawn chair from the barn," she called over her shoulder.

By the time Tom got to the paddock, Olivia had the chair waiting for him, and she was already perched on the top rail of the paddock fence. As he lowered himself slowly into the chair, she started to play a soft melody on her harmonica. Sonny ignored them, but Nanny and Bud immediately came out of the barn and followed the haunting sounds of the harmonica toward Olivia. Nanny lay down next to the fence, and Bud rested his big head against Olivia's leg.

Tom smiled at the effect the music had on the two animals. "Come on, Sonny," he whispered. "You know you want to join us." He reached in his pocket and pulled out some of the peppermints Jan Taylor had given him. He unwrapped three of them and held out his hand first to Bud and then to Nanny. Next, he pushed himself up from the chair, and balancing on one foot, he laid one on the rail of the fence. He watched intently as Sonny cautiously began moving closer to them. "Here he comes," he whispered softly to

Olivia. "Don't move and keep playing."

Slowly and cautiously Sonny took a few steps and then stopped. "Come on, fellow," Olivia heard her dad whisper again. She continued to play and sat as still as she possibly could.

Tom held his breath, hoping something didn't spoil the moment. This was truly a breakthrough for all of them.

Bud turned around to look at Sonny and then moved quietly away from the fence and the unwrapped peppermint laying on the top rail close to Olivia. It was almost as if he was providing space for the young horse to join them. Nanny raised her head and bleated softly, encouraging Sonny to come closer.

Ever so vigilant, Sonny moved toward them. Finally, he stopped just in front of Olivia. A cool, evening breeze gently blew across the paddock, carrying with it the scent of the peppermint. Sonny looked toward the fence, quickly stretched out his neck, and pulled the peppermint into his mouth with his lips.

Neither Tom nor Olivia moved or tried to touch him. Tears of joy streamed down Olivia's cheeks as she began to play *Keep Your Eyes on Heaven*.

After several minutes, Sonny let out a big sigh and dropped his head. In the moonlight, Tom could see the tensed muscles in the young colts neck and body begin to soften and relax. The first step toward a trusting relationship had just been completed. "Thank God," Tom whispered, and

Olivia just smiled.

Chapter 8

The alarm went off the next morning at 4:30, and Olivia quickly jumped out of bed. Jan had called the cabin last night and had invited her to go over to the Triple Bar Ranch with her this morning to help them out for a while. She had also invited them to some party on Saturday night. Olivia had begged her dad not to make her go to the party, but he insisted. As usual, he won the argument.

She hurriedly splashed her face with cold water, brushed her teeth, and pulled her hair back with her old rubber band. She dressed quickly and headed down the stairs. She was surprised to find her dad already up and breakfast on the table.

"What are you doing up so early, Dad?" she asked. She grabbed a piece of toast from the stack on the table and leaned over to kiss him on the top of the head.

"I'm in training," replied Tom. "I'll soon be starting to work with Sonny by this time every morning."

Olivia plopped down on her chair and reached for the platter of scrambled eggs. She took two large scoops of eggs on her plate and then reached for the bacon and hash browns. "How's this all going to work out with you training Sonny and me helping out at the Triple Bar?"

"Jan said they'll be working their horses out at night when the summer heat hits."

"Why?" asked Olivia gulping down a large drink of orange juice.

"I'd guess they probably have too many horses to work in the morning and can't get them all ridden before the sun starts heating up."

"Hmm," said Olivia. "I guess that'll work. I can help them out at night and then help you in the morning. It'll be like working a third shift job at least until we leave for Ruidoso."

Tom hesitated for a minute and then replied, "Olivia, you're going to have to tell me if it turns out you like working with the horses at the Triple Bar better'n you like helping out with Sonny. It'll be your choice."

"My choice, huh? Why is it, you'll let me choose some things, but you won't let me decide about this party thing?"

Tom chuckled. "Well, it's just that about some things you're level headed and others you're not."

"I've gotta go," she said jumping up from the table. "I don't want to be late on my first day. Just stack the dishes in the sink. I'll take care of them when I get home."

"Hey," said Tom, "I made the mess; I'll do the clean up. Just watch yourself over there and don't be late getting back. We're going to town as soon as you get home to shop for something for you to wear Saturday night."

"You really are going to make me put on a dress and go to

that stupid party, aren't you?"

"Sure am," said Tom. "Have a nice day," he called.

Olivia looked over and stuck her tongue out at him. When she went out the door, she was surprised to see Bud already saddled and tied to the railing of the front steps. "You even saddled Bud?" she called through the screen door. "What time *did* you get up, anyway?"

Tom grabbed his crutches and limped to the door. "Like I told you," he said. "I'm in training. You just don't remember what working with race horses was like. It's a heck of a lot different from bull ridin' in rodeos."

"It must be," said Olivia. "I used to have to pull you out of the truck at noon."

"I never had any reason to get up back then," he said.

Olivia turned around and smiled at him. "Well, you do now; that's for sure," she said.

~~~~~~

Justin couldn't believe his eyes as he watched his Aunt Jan ride up with Olivia. He glared at Jan with a look that made her squirm a bit in her saddle.

"Justin, I believe you met Olivia Blake the other day," Jan said casually.

"How's your head?" teased Olivia.

69

Justin turned his back and stormed into the barn.

"Oops," said Olivia. "I guess I'd better not tease him anymore about fainting."

"Yeah, it would probably be a good idea not to bring that up again," said Jan winking at Olivia. "Come on. The first thing we need to do is round up some of the calves we'll use this morning for training. Are you comfortable enough on Bud to do that?"

"Sure," said Olivia. "Just lead the way."

For the next half-hour, the three of them isolated and penned the calves they needed. Jan was impressed with how easily Olivia maintained her balance in the saddle, allowing Bud to have his head and work the cow. "You're a natural," she called to Olivia.

"Thanks. That was great fun," Olivia responded. She glanced toward Justin, but it was obvious he wasn't going to pay her any compliment.

"I'll work the chestnut mare next," he said as he rode past the two women.

"Come on, Olivia," said Jan trying to make up for Justin's rudeness. "I'll show you around the barn, so you'll be able to find everything. It's going to save us a lot of time having you saddle and bathe the horses."

"Are you sure it's all right for me to be here?" asked Olivia.

"Justin seems more than a little put out because I'm here."

"He's always a grump in the morning," said Jan. "I'm sure he'll warm up in an hour or so."

"I'm not so sure that's all there is to his attitude," said Olivia. "Was this his idea to have me help out?"

"You certainly are a perceptive young woman." Jan chuckled. "To be honest with you, it was my idea, but I have no doubt Justin will come on board after he sees how much time he'll save with you helping him out. Just ignore him right now."

"Well OK, if you say so, but he sure has a burr up his butt."

"You are so right," Jan replied laughing.

For the next three hours, Olivia was kept busy bathing and saddling horses. She didn't have much time to watch Jan and Justin work in the arena, which was disappointing to her, but she hoped that would eventually change.

"Look at that, Justin," chided Jan as they rode into the barn after working the last two horses. "We're finished two whole hours earlier than usual. Why don't you take Olivia into the arena and show her some of the basic reining patterns?"

If looks actually *could* kill, Jan realized Justin's stare would have meant instant death for her.

"I'm sure Olivia has other things to do to help out her dad," snarled Justin.

"No, I don't, not really," quickly responded Olivia. "Right now, Sonny's not ready to work. Dad's just trying to build up a little trust with him, and Sonny's beginning to come around."

"Why don't you see what the gray mare is able to do with reining since we already decided she wasn't good as a cow horse?" suggested Jan looking at Justin.

"You're the reining champion," he answered. "Why don't you work with Olivia?"

"I would, but I have to be over at the recording studio at noon to listen to the new cuts we made earlier this week." Jan glared at Justin with a look that dared him to deny her request.

Justin realized his aunt was not going to take *no* for an answer. "OK. Fine," he muttered. "Saddle up the gray mare in the last stall in the second aisle."

"Olivia, you go ahead and saddle the mare. I'll wash down my horse," said Jan.

"I don't know how to thank you," gushed Olivia turning to face Justin. "I would really like to try my hand at reining."

Justin rolled his eyes and swung his horse around toward the arena.

Olivia quickly saddled the mare and headed out of the

barn. When she opened the gate to let herself into the arena, Justin rode up to her. "Just watch me work the pattern, then I'll see what you can do with the mare," he said abruptly.

"Wait a minute, Justin," responded Olivia. "If I've done something to offend you, I'm sorry. And if you'd rather not do this, just tell me, and I'll leave." She glanced up at him with an apologetic look.

Justin looked down at her and felt a twinge of guilt at the way he had treated her all morning. Finally, he muttered, "No, stay. I'm going to need some help with working the reining horses anyway as soon as Aunt Jan starts on her tour. If it turns out you can handle it that would be a lot of help."

Olivia swallowed back tears she couldn't explain. "Thanks," she muttered. "Like you, Justin, working with horses has been my life, and I hope it will also be my future. I want to learn as much about them and about how to work with them as I can."

Justin stared into her bright, blue eyes now brimming with tears that threatened to spill over and cascade down her cheeks. He felt a strange sensation in the pit of his stomach. "Well, then," he stammered, "let's get started."

For the next two hours, Olivia carefully observed and followed Justin's directions.

"Great," shouted Justin over and over again. He was totally blown away by how quickly she learned the patterns and by how easily she led the gray mare through them. Olivia and the mare seemed to be a perfect pair with each trying the best they could to impress him. He couldn't believe he was looking at the same lazy horse that he had seen yesterday.

After the workout, Justin helped Olivia wash down their two horses. They laughed and enjoyed one another's company with no sign of the former animosity between them. As she was leaving, Olivia turned around in Bud's saddle and called to Justin, "See you tomorrow, OK?"

"You bet," he said, smiling broadly. "Wait" he called, "did my Aunt Jan tell you about the graduation party tomorrow night?"

"Yeah, she did," said Olivia, heaving a deep sigh.

"What?" asked Justin. "You're going to come, aren't you?"

"Do I have to wear a dress?"

Justin laughed. "Hey, wear whatever you want to—just come," he said.

Olivia smiled. "I'll be there," she called back at him, "although you probably won't recognize me, and just know I'm going to feel completely miserable without my jeans and flannel shirt."

Chapter 9

Olivia stood before the full-length mirror in her bedroom and scarcely recognized the reflection staring back at her. She turned around and glanced over her shoulder to make sure the tag on the back of her white, silk peasant blouse wasn't sticking out. "Hmm," she said, "I guess I look all right, but I certainly don't feel like me. At least I still have on boots." She wiggled her feet back and forth inside of her new Tony Lama boots. "But even they don't feel right," she moaned.

She stepped away from the mirror and reached up under her mid-calf denim skirt to pull down the off-the-shoulder peasant blouse, so it was smoothly tucked around the waistline of her skirt. Grabbing the narrow, metallic silver and gold braided belt from the bed, she fastened it around her tiny waist, allowing the silver tipped point of the belt to drape down across her flat stomach.

Her skirt was split in the front, exposing her boots and her lower legs. "Geez, my legs are as pale as ghosts," she moaned. "Of course, they've rarely seen the light of day." She pushed the sides of her hair back from her face. "Now I know why I always wear this mob of curls back in a pony tail. It's always in my eyes." She never wore her hair down and loose, but she decided that tonight she would wear it like Jan Taylor wore hers.

Grabbing the silver hoop earrings from the top of the small writing desk and her new silk wrap from the chair, she headed down the steps.

"Wow," greeted her dad. "Look at you. You're an absolute knock out. I wasn't sure you actually had legs."

"Ha, ha," mocked Olivia. "You're looking mighty spiffy yourself in your white, western shirt and new jeans. You're even sporting the prize winning, silver belt buckle you won five years ago as the World Champion Bull Rider. I don't think I've ever seen you wear it before."

"You don't think it's too much, do you?" asked Tom uncertainly. "I know it's old."

"No. It's perfect," assured Olivia. "You rode a lot of bulls to earn that little piece of silver and gold. You should wear it all the time."

Tom reached in his pocket. "Here," he said as he handed her a short, silver chain with a delicate, turquoise heart medallion dangling from it. "I thought this would look nice with the neckline of your blouse."

Olivia's eyes filled with tears. "It's perfect, Dad," she said hugging him tightly around the neck. "Here, put it on for me." She turned around and lifted her hair off the back of her neck.

"I'm glad you wore your hair down," said Tom as he draped the necklace around her neck. "You've got gorgeous curls. I've always been a little sorry you keep them slicked back with that ugly red, rubber band."

"Well, don't get use to it," responded Olivia. "It drives me nuts falling every which way around my face."

"Well, anyway. I'm glad you're wearing it loose tonight," he said again.

Olivia sighed. "Let's get this over with," she called over her shoulder as she headed out the screen door.

~~~~~~~~~~~~

When they arrived at the Triple Bar Ranch, a large crowd was milling around in the lovely, outdoor verandah, and a local band was playing from a stage at the far end of the patio. "So much for worrying about me being isolated from other people," whispered Olivia as she grabbed hold of her dad's arm. "Don't you dare leave me alone," she pleaded.

Tom reached over and patted his daughter's hand. "Relax, darlin'," he assured. "I don't doubt for a minute that I'll be the one left on my own. Just smile and act like you're the belle of the ball."

"I don't know how to do that," she groaned.

Justin's best friend, Frank Blaney, spotted Olivia from across the patio. "Wow, who is that? She's the most gorgeous thing I've seen around here for a long time," he muttered under his breath.

Justin turned around to see who he was looking at and could hardly believe his eyes. He would never have recognized Olivia if she hadn't been clinging to her dad's arm.

"Please, tell me that she's not married to that worn out looking cowboy she's with," said Frank.

"Take it easy, Frank," warned Justin resenting the way Frank was gazing at Olivia. "That's Olivia Blake and her dad. He's the new trainer Brett hired to train Raven's Son."

"Thank goodness. See you later," said Frank as he darted across the patio toward Olivia.

Jan and Brett spotted the Blakes as they headed toward a table at the edge of the patio. "Come on, Brett. Let's go and get them to join us," suggested Jan. "They look absolutely miserable."

"Hey, you two," called Brett motioning for the Blakes to join them at their table. "I almost didn't recognize you, old man," he said slapping Tom lightly across the shoulders. "And look at you Olivia—clean face and all," he teased.

"You look absolutely stunning, Olivia," said Jan.

"Thanks, Mrs. Kendall," Olivia muttered.

"Mrs. Kendall? What happened to you calling me Jan?"

"I'm sorry," said Olivia blushing. "I just thought it was being too familiar in public to call you Jan."

"While I love being Mrs. Kendall," said Jan hugging Olivia around the shoulders, "I prefer to be called Jan—especially by my friends."

"Excuse me," interrupted Frank. "I don't think we've had the chance to meet," he said staring at Olivia. "I'm Frank Blaney, a friend of Justin's."

"Hey, Olivia," said Justin as he brushed Frank aside. "Why don't you come with me, so I can introduce you to some of my relatives and friends?" He took Olivia possessively by the hand and pulled her away from Frank and the others.

Frank frowned and took off after them.

Jan and Tom looked at each other and smiled. "Well, we probably won't be seeing much more of Olivia tonight," said Jan.

"I thought you said Justin was bringing a date tonight?" commented Brett.

"He said he was, but I guess he didn't," said Jan laughing. "At least, I hope he wouldn't be that rude to some poor girl. It's obvious he and Frank are going to square off and compete for Olivia's attention the rest of the night."

Tom heaved a sigh of relief. He was proud of his young daughter and felt he had finally managed to help her become the beautiful, young woman he wanted her to be. Now all he had to worry about was keeping the young men from grabbing her away from him before he was ready to give her up.

Chapter 10

Tom walked out into the crisp, morning breeze. He glanced toward the east as the sun was just peeking over the top of the horizon. The sky was a rainbow of colors of deep purple, mulberry, and pale green, blue, and yellow. He inhaled deeply, filling his lungs with the sweet smell of Texas bluebonnets. He was pleased with the world today because of the excitement Olivia had experienced last night. She had babbled continuously on their way home from Justin's party about the marvelous people she had met and about how much fun it had been to dance the two-step with so many of Justin's friends. He smiled as he thought about what a beautiful, young woman she was in every way. She was as sweet and sincere as a child, and last night, she proved she could be as beautiful and refined as any young debutante at her first cotillion.

As he headed toward the barn, Tom noticed Sonny standing motionless in the paddock and silhouetted in the dim light of the early dawn. He stood still for several minutes, quietly admiring the noble looking horse. Although he was only a two-year-old, Sonny was an impressive long-legged, smooth muscled horse with a slender frame and strong hindquarters and powerful legs. He was already sixteen hands, and he hadn't stopped growing. From a distance, Sonny could easily have been mistaken for his majestic sire, Raven.

He watched Sonny quietly take a long drink and decided this was an opportunity that he might not get again once the heat of the day would force the animals to stay in their stalls. He moved slowly toward the fence, whistling softly. Sonny turned his proud, defiant head toward the sound and pawed the ground nervously. Tom leaned his crutches against the rail of the fence, and with considerable effort, he managed to climb to the top rail by balancing himself with his uninjured leg and hopping up on one rail at a time, until he was finally able to swing his cast over the top rail. Sonny kept a watchful eye on him but didn't move toward him.

Once settled on the top rail, Tom began to speak softly to Sonny. "Good morning, little fellow," he called to the horse. "I'm glad to see you're an early riser, too. You know, we've got a lot to do in a short amount of time here. It would sure help out if you would be a little more cooperative."

Sonny made a soft blowing sound, and Tom studied him carefully. He knew that when a horse blows through his nose with his mouth closed, he is signaling he is curious about something. If, after making the blowing sound, the horse appears relaxed and calm, it's an indication he's simply willing to check things out and doesn't sense any need to be on alert. On the other hand, if the blowing sound is immediately followed by the horse becoming tense, it signals he senses danger, and as a prey animal, he is immediately ready either to charge into a fight or to take flight. Sonny stopped pawing at the ground and simply turned his head toward Tom as if he was still trying to decide how he felt about him.

Tom moved his hand slowly into his pocket and pulled out a wrapped peppermint. He rattled the paper of the candy to watch Sonny's reaction. Again, he heard the soft blowing sound, but there was a little more visible tension in Sonny's body this time. *Maybe he's just excited about the candy*, thought Tom. Slowly, he unwrapped the peppermint and dropped it into his hand. Stealthily, he stretched his hand out with the candy resting on his upturned palm. He sat motionless, simply waiting for Sonny to choose what would happen next.

Sonny turned around until he was fully facing Tom. He raised his head and whinnied loudly as if he were calling to someone or something. Bud immediately wandered out into the paddock and stood by his rear stall door. Nanny peeked her head around the corner of Sonny's stall and looked first at Sonny and then at Tom. Seeing nothing to be worried about, she just bleated softly and went back inside of the barn. Bud made a low nickering sound, seeming to provide reassurance to Sonny.

"See, little fellow," whispered Tom in a low, assuring tone. "It's okay. I'm not going to hurt you," he soothed.

Sonny dropped his head and cautiously moved toward Tom and the peppermint. Tom held his breath afraid a bird or sudden movement would frighten the reluctant horse. Finally, Sonny got close enough to Tom that he could reach out and take the candy, but he didn't. He just stood there, gazing at Tom as if he were trying to see through to his soul. "It's okay," Tom assured again. "I won't hurt you," he repeated. "I just want to help you show the world how magnificent you are."

Sonny hesitated, but he finally stretched his neck out

and quickly sucked the peppermint into his mouth. As he munched on the candy, he made no attempt to move away but simply remained still, staring at Tom. Tom slowly stretched his hand out again and placed it gently next to Sonny's nostrils, allowing him to sniff his hand as a way of sharing a friendly greeting between horse and man.

Olivia quietly watched the scene in the paddock from her bedroom window. "Mission accomplished," she muttered as she watched her dad cautiously stroke Sonny on the neck. She was thrilled for her dad because now he could start working with Sonny to begin his training for the Ruidoso Futurity, but she also felt a twinge of deep sadness. If her dad was going to have Sonny ready for the first leg of the Triple Crown in May, he would have to take him to Ruidoso a month or so before the actual race to condition him to the change in elevation and weather in New Mexico. That would mean she would also have to leave Texas. With schooling races and other smaller races, they would probably be gone off and on most of the summer until Labor Day and the actual running of the All American Futurity.

She moved away from the window and sat down on the side of the bed, trying to decide what it was she actually wanted to do. A few days ago, she would have been jumping for joy that they might actually have a chance to train and race Sonny. Now she wasn't certain that traipsing across the country with no real place to call home was what she wanted. She exhaled a deep, long sigh that seemed to come from the very pits of her soul. Slowly, she got up and headed into the bathroom. *This is dad's last chance*, she thought. *I still have my whole life ahead of me.* It was clear now what she would do.

Chapter 11

The next several weeks went by in a blur for Olivia. From midnight to four every day, she went to the Triple Bar Ranch to help Justin and Jan. Then she would rush back to the Kendall Ranch to help her dad with Sonny every morning, and finally she would collapse into bed by noon. She now had routine in her life, but it was exhausting.

In the evening, the heat and humidity of the hot Texas days would slowly release their suffocating grasp and give way to a cool, evening breeze and the brilliance of the moon in the star studded, cloudless sky. Each night, Justin would ride over to meet her before they started their nightly training, and they would ride back to the Triple Bar together across the wide, open plains between the two ranches. She loved the evening rides with him. Sometimes they would talk to each other about all sorts of topics as they rode along. Other times, they would just ride silently across the dusty lowland and enjoy the gentle touch of the soft breeze against their skin and the spectacular light show above them.

Sonny was slowly adjusting to his new routine too. Every morning when Olivia returned from the Triple Bar, Tom would have him ready, so Olivia and Bud could pony him across the vast acreage for his morning exercise. On these outings, Olivia would alter their pace, transitioning between slow walks, easy jogs, and short sprints. Before and after every exercise session, Tom would carefully run his trained hands down Sonny's legs and across his body, feeling for any signs of increased heat or swelling. Depending on what he discovered through his careful examination, Tom would give Olivia strict instructions about the exercise regimen relative to the distance, speed, and gait he wanted her to follow.

Almost immediately, Olivia could see the results of the ponying exercises in terms of Sonny's increased speed and stamina. At the end of their morning runs, Tom would bathe him, and Olivia would walk him around the paddock until his breathing was relaxed. Occasionally, Tom would use the mechanical walker to cool Sonny down, but he preferred to have Olivia do the cool down, so he could watch Sonny's movements and track the amount of time it would take his vital signs to return to normal. After his cool down, Sonny would be returned to his stall where he would enjoy a breakfast of fresh alfalfa, clean water, and enriched grains. He would spend the rest of the day inside of the fan-cooled barn protected from the Texas heat.

Though she enjoyed the ponying exercises, Olivia couldn't wait to climb on Sonny's back and begin the real exercise routines that would eventually prepare him to sprint out of a starting gate and run at top speed for the required distance that, for quarter horse races, is measured in yards. For Sonny, as a two-year-old, the distance for the All American Futurity was 440 yards or a quarter mile—the distance that gave the Quarter Horse its name. Last year's winner of the Futurity ran that distance in just over twenty-one seconds. Olivia knew the American Quarter Horse was the fastest horse in the world, even faster than the thoroughbred. Speeds of up to fifty-five miles per hour were documented for the American Quarter Horse.

The thrill of sitting atop a paper-thin saddle and going from a standing start to over forty miles per hour in just a few strides was something Olivia longed to experience. She knew Sonny had the speed to give her that thrill, and all she had to do was to convince her dad and Brett Kendall that she had the strength, stamina, and courage to compete in such a fast-paced race—a race dominated primarily by males.

For the most part, their morning exercise routine was uneventful except for an occasional surprise caused by an unexpected deer suddenly darting across in front of them or a low flying eagle swooping toward them. When these interruptions occurred, Sonny was still a little skittish. Sometimes he would rear or try to pull away from Olivia, but she had learned from her dad to keep the lead line wrapped around the horn of her saddle.

This morning, both Sonny and Bud appeared to be a little restless as they were getting ready to leave the barn. The weather had changed, and there was a prediction of a storm headed their way. All the ranchers were hoping the storm would bring with it the rain they so desperately needed. Their pasture lands were turning into acres of dust, and the creek and river beds were nothing but parched gulches. If the drought continued, they would be forced to sell off their herds before they were fatted, and they would bring significantly lower than average prices. Such economic hardships would bankrupt many of the ranches. Justin had shared with her last night the threat to his own family's ranch in such difficult economic times.

Like most folks who absent mindedly go to the grocery store and who heedlessly complain about higher costs, Olivia had not given much previous thought to the hardships farmers and ranchers face with the challenges the weather can cause. While city residents may complain the weather interferes with their picnics and other outdoor plans, the weather can actually destroy the basic livelihood of ranchers and farmers. It is the chaos the weather creates that starts the vicious cycle of higher prices due to diminishing supply. And as more and more farmers and ranchers are forced to abandon their fields and pastures and more ranch and farmlands are gobbled up by developers, the cost of food will always continue to rise.

"Olivia," said Tom. "Keep your eyes on the sky this morning and don't go too far away in case there's a sudden storm. Right now it seems like it will be just another hot, Texas day, but these storms can come up quickly."

"Okay, Dad. Don't worry," she called over her shoulder as she headed out to the open land behind the barn.

At first, the horses willingly responded to her cues to head away from the barn, but as they got farther away, even Bud resisted her demands to move forward. Finally, when they got near the bottom of the ridge that stretched across the border of the two ranches, Bud came to a complete stop, refusing to move at all.

Sonny reared and pulled back on the lead line. "What's

wrong with you two?" yelled Olivia. She glanced toward the morning sky in front of her, and there was no sign of a storm, but she did notice that suddenly the gentle morning breeze had become stronger, causing the dust to blow up into her eyes. She turned around in the saddle and looked to the left above the ridge. And then, she saw it.

"Oh my god," she yelled, but the roar from the approaching swirling, snake-like cloud coming across the peak of the ridge swallowed her voice. Both horses nervously pranced in tight circles, and she was barely able to keep Bud from racing away from the horrendous noise. They were suddenly being pummeled with small bits of rock, twigs, hard rain, and hail stone. Dirt stirred by the fierce winds stung her face and hands and blew into her eyes.

She anxiously looked around her for somewhere to go to get away from the violently swirling mass hanging down from an enormous black cloud above it, but they were quite alone in the wide open plains. She jumped down from the saddle and pulled Bud toward a dark spot ahead of them at the foot of the ridge. Silently she prayed it was a gap between the rocks that would be large enough for the three of them to fit into. As she struggled to pull the two horses forward, Sonny continued to rear and pull against the lead line tied to the saddle. Just as they reached the spot she was hoping would be their refuge, the snap on Sonny's halter broke, and the frightened horse sped away from them and from the insidious roar.

Planting her heels in the ground and clinging tightly to Bud's reins, it was all she could do to keep him from darting after Sonny. She and Bud stared helplessly at the dark horse racing away from the chaos and disappearing in clouds of dust. Finally, she managed to pull Bud into the large crevice between the rocks, as the storm swept by above them. Together they hovered in the darkness. Bud was shaking all over, and tears were streaming down her face, but if either of them was making any noise at all, the sound was lost in the winds and pelting hail against the rocks.

Then, as quickly as it had started, the storm was over. The rain and hail slowed then stopped altogether as the winds diminished, and daylight replaced the darkness. Once she was sure the worst of the storm had passed, Olivia carefully pushed Bud backward out of the cramped quarters that had saved them from the ravaging tornado. There was no sign of the ominous cloud that had apparently disappeared on the other side of the rocky rise. Quickly, she swung herself into the saddle and raced Bud in the direction where they had last seen Sonny running from the storm.

They flew past small, uprooted trees and pieces of metal probably lifted off one of the barns on the Triple Bar or Kendall ranches. Olivia pushed aside any thoughts of the possible destruction the storm might have caused to the buildings on the ranches in the area and of the potential injuries that might have occurred to the ranchers and animals. She knew there were storm cellars at both ranches and at the log cabin. She prayed her dad and the others had been able to reach them before the storm hit.

When they arrived near the edge of the Triple Bar ranch,

Olivia could see another horse and rider racing toward her. As they drew closer, she recognized Justin.

"Thank God," he said when he finally caught up with her. "I was afraid you had been hurt or carried away by the storm. I knew you'd be out here exercising Sonny."

"I lost him," she blurted out as tears streamed down her cheeks. "His halter snap broke, and he just took off running in front of the storm."

Justin jumped off his horse and caught her as she slid down from Bud. "I tried," she cried. "I really tried to lead both of them to a shelter among the rocks, but he just broke away, and I couldn't do anything," she sobbed as she fell into Justin's arms.

"We'll find him," he assured. "Unless the fences were blown down or he climbs over the top of the ridge, he's has to be somewhere on one of the ranches. But thank goodness, you're okay." He hugged her tightly and rocked her gently from side to side until she stopped crying.

"I'm sorry," she muttered. "I was so scared for all of you and my dad." Abruptly, she pulled away from Justin. "My dad," she screeched. "I've got to go check on my dad."

Justin pulled his cell phone out of his back pocket. "Shoot, no bars out here. We'd better go back to the cabin first. The tornado didn't actually touch the ground, so it looks like there was minimal damage to our ranch. Hopefully, that's true for the Kendall ranch too. We were lucky this time."

Justin helped Olivia back into the saddle. "I know your dad must be worried sick, so we'll let him know you're okay, and then we can organize a hunting party for Sonny."

On their way back to the Kendall Ranch, they spotted Brett and Tom racing along the foot of the ridge in the four-wheeler. Justin took off toward them and eventually attracted their attention. When they reached Olivia, Tom hopped out of the four-wheeler on one leg and literally pulled her off Bud into his arms. Tears streamed from his eyes as he hugged her. "Thank God. Thank God," he repeated over and over.

Olivia tried to soothe him. "Dad, I'm okay. I'm okay," she consoled. "Only," she said hesitantly, "I lost Sonny. He broke loose from me, and he's gone. I'm truly sorry, Mr. Kendall," she said gently pulling away from her dad and turning toward Brett. "I tried to hang on to him, but the snap on the halter broke, and he went racing across the lowland ahead of the storm," she said pointing to the north.

Brett walked around the four-wheeler and put his arm around Olivia's shoulders. "It was you that we were most worried about. We'll find that crazy horse," he comforted her. "I'm just glad you weren't hurt."

"I was able to pull Bud into a crevice I spotted in the rocks, and it sheltered us from most of the storm."

"Look," said Justin pointing toward a cloud of dust in the distance.

They all turned to see what Justin was pointing to. "It's Sonny," shouted Olivia.

Bud put his head up high in the air and whinnied so loudly the others were forced to cover their ears. Sonny suddenly changed direction and came running toward them.

"Look at that horse run," yelled Tom and Brett simultaneously.

"Man, he's coming fast," said Justin.

"We definitely have us a race horse," said Brett, slapping Tom on the shoulder.

"You sure do," said Justin. "Now all you need is to find someone who can stay on him."

"That'll be me," announced Olivia. "I can ride him. I know I can."

The three men turned to stare at her, and she could see the surprise and disappointment in Justin's eyes.

"I want to ride him," she proclaimed firmly as she rode off to greet the distraught colt and to lead him toward the security of his paddock.

Chapter 12

As soon as Olivia managed to get Sonny back inside the paddock after his race against the storm, Tom examined him carefully. Not only did he want to make sure he hadn't sustained any severe external injuries, he also checked to see if Sonny was showing any signs of tying up, a condition prevalent among overworked horses. When a horse is worked hard or long, the horse's body produces higher levels of lactate than can be naturally absorbed, which causes the animal's muscles to stay in a constant state of contraction. Similar to the pain of the charley-horse humans feel, such a condition generates considerable pain for the horse and can debilitate him for weeks when such contractions fail to relax thus tying up the muscles. Tom knew Sonny was fit from the consistent exercise regimen they had been doing with him, and he was well-bred—two qualities that would help ward off tying up. On the other hand, young horses as high strung as Sonny are more prone to tie up.

Other than a few scratches and tiny cuts, most likely caused by blowing debris during the storm, Tom was relieved to find Sonny didn't appear to have any visible injuries. It was internal damage such as the potential of skeletal, muscular, and pulmonary injuries that worried him the most. If Sonny had been continuously running during the entire time between when he broke loose from Olivia and when they found him, muscles in his legs could have become fatigued. When this happens, horses can easily overextend a tendon, which can lead to a bowing of the tendon or even to bone fractures. Fatigued muscles can also lead to pulmonary hemorrhaging and other circulatory problems.

As of now, Sonny didn't show any signs of bleeding from the mouth or nostrils, which also provided some relief for Tom, but he knew that tomorrow might bring different warnings of Sonny's condition.

"He seems to be okay," reported Tom. "But it may be a few days before we'll really know if he has sustained any serious internal injuries. My chance with him can easily have blown away in that storm."

"I'm sorry, Dad. I really did try to lead him into the cavern, but the snap broke."

"Olivia, honey, no one is blaming you for this. You obviously used your head in finding somewhere for you and Bud to escape from the storm. I would never trade a single hair on your head for the chance to work with Sonny. Surely you know that for heaven's sake." He reached over and put his arm around Olivia. "But we do need to have a conversation about you racing him. I'm not in favor of that at all."

"Why not?" asked Olivia. "Sonny's already refused to be ridden by some of the best jockeys in the business. He's learning to trust me, and I know I can do it. I'm below the height and weight maximums, and you know I'm not afraid to compete in a man's world. I don't understand your reluctance about this."

"My objections are not based on your lack of skill, honey. I know you can ride any horse out there. But there's a lot more at stake in racing than in the rodeo circuit."

"Other than prize money, what else are you talking about?"

Tom stopped brushing Sonny and pitched the brush into his tack box. He turned to look directly at Olivia. "The money does make a big difference, and that's the reason for the other dangers in racing. Jockeys earn their living by winning, not by just running the race."

"Jockeys are paid a mounting fee regardless of whether they win or lose," protested Olivia, "so I still don't understand what you're getting at."

Tom started walking back to the barn with Sonny, and Olivia ran to catch up with him. "You're right, Olivia. Jockeys do get a mount fee, but it's not enough for them to live on. They rely on their percentage of the race purses to support themselves and their families. To get the best mounts, they have to have a winning record as a jockey. It's a vicious circle—they have to win to earn rides on winning horses—so they fight pretty hard to be up there in the top five. Jockeys may be best friends off the track, but on the track, it's all about winning. They all need to win and don't think for a moment they'll cut you any slack just because you're a woman."

"I certainly don't need them to cut me any slack," said Olivia. "I'm able to compete on their level, and I intend to be out in front the entire way, so you won't have to worry about them bumping me around."

96

Tom laughed. "Sweetie, you haven't even a clue about how hard it will be to get to the front. It's that dash to the front where all the bumping and tousling around happens. Don't forget Quarter Horse racing is a drag race where you're expected to drive your horse from zero to more than forty miles per hour in just a few strides and keep that pace for 440 yards."

"Don't you think I know that? I can do this, Dad. I want to do this," Olivia insisted.

Tom shook his head. "Is this really what you want to do for *you*? Or, is this what you want to do for me?" He tossed her a plastic scoop and pointed to the grain barrel.

Olivia lifted off the lid of the barrel and filled the scoop to the top with the grain. She poured the grain into Sonny's feed bucket then turned to look at her dad. "I want to do this for both of us."

"Olivia, honey, you've been taking care of me for a long time, and I think it's time for me to take care of myself. I know you like the training and riding you're doing with Jan and Justin. Unfortunately, sweetie, you can't do both. They're in it to win too, and they can't have you popping in and out of their regimen any more than I can have you only working part-time with Sonny and me."

Olivia stared at him in silence.

Tom reached out and put his arm around her shoulders and pulled her close to him. "Personally, Olivia, I would feel a lot better about you working with Justin and participating in performance competitions than I would having you race against ten to fifteen jockeys whose sole aim is to make sure you don't get in front of them."

Olivia drew in a deep breath and plopped down on a bale of hay. "Honestly, Dad, I'm not sure what I want. I like both types of competition, and I think I could be successful at either one. But what I do know is that I like sitting atop of a speeding horse better than anything. Racing can give me that thrill; reining can't."

"You've never raced against a pack of speeding horses, Olivia. Racing's a lot more than just holding onto the mane of a speeding horse."

"I know that, but you can teach me how to get out in front of the pack. I know you can."

Tom sat down next to Olivia on the hay. "But you're missing my point. I don't *want* to teach you how to get in front of a pack of riders and horses intent on taking you out of the race. It's too dangerous. I don't want to be the one who teaches you something that could end up crippling you or even killing you. I won't do it, and that's final."

"Dad, I know the odds. I've looked them up. There's typically one death each year among jockeys, but there are more than twenty deaths from horse related accidents annually, so my odds are really better on the racetrack."

Tom stared at her for a moment and then grabbed his crutches and started toward the barn door. "I don't want to talk about this anymore," he finally muttered. "Anyway, we aren't the only ones who'll make this decision. Brett Kendall will also have to be involved in the decision."

"But if you tell him I can handle Sonny, he'll let me have a chance to prove myself. I know he will."

He turned to stare at her. "Please, Olivia, let's go celebrate the fact we're both still in one piece after that storm and find out if others were as lucky as us."

Olivia stared at him and then shouted, "This conversation isn't over. I'm the best jockey for Sonny, and you know it."

Tom knew there was no sense of arguing. She was right. In his heart, he knew she would be the best jockey for Sonny given his hot disposition, but he certainly didn't want to expose his daughter to the dangers of racing, even if it meant winning.

Chapter 13

The Triple Bar and Kendall ranches were among the lucky ones that managed to escape the ravaging destruction of the tornado. Ranches on the other side of the ridge were not as fortunate. As it crossed to the southern side, the tornado touched down and cut a path of destruction a mile wide and three miles long. The death toll of the tornado in the area was reported at six, and losses to homes, businesses, and livestock were estimated at well over a million dollars. Jan immediately had Roger organize a concert at Luchenbach to raise money for the families hardest hit by the storm. Everyone from the Triple Bar and Kendall ranches and their neighbors, the Fletchers, volunteered to work at the concert, so all the proceeds could go to the victims of the storm.

Olivia was amazed at how quickly everything was accomplished. With the help of Jan's blog, other social media outlets, and free radio, TV, and newspaper ads, news of the concert spread across Texas, Oklahoma, and beyond. Having just won the *Entertainer of the Year Award*, Jan had fans from all over who were determined to support her by flocking to the tiny town where the acreage for parking surrounding it was considerably larger than the actual town itself. On the day of the concert, Olivia rode to Luchenbach with Justin and his sister Jamie. Hours before the concert was to begin, cars, RVs, and motorcycles were already pouring into the parking grounds surrounding the historic town.

"Justin, why don't you show Olivia around the town," suggested Jamie, "while I meet with the concert organizers. I'll catch up with you later at the stage."

"Good idea," said Justin. "Come on, Olivia."

Olivia knew little about Luchenbach except for what she had read on the Internet. She had never been here before and was immediately enthralled with its history. When they walked down the unpaved, only street in the town, they were greeted by free roaming chickens and one proud rooster. Huge oak trees in front of one of the only two buildings in town provided shade from the heat of the day. *Rustic* was the only word Olivia could think of to describe Luchenbach, but she wasn't even sure it captured its roughly preserved antiquity. She paused to read the historical marker that stood in front of the Engel home at the edge of the tiny town. August Engel was an itinerant preacher from Germany, and his family is given credit for Luchenbach's founding in the mid 1800's. The nine acre town was first called Grape Creek, but when the Engels applied for a town post office, they changed the name on the application to Luchenbach, the last name of the fiancé of Engel's daughter, Minna.

"Interesting little place, isn't it?" said Justin.

"It's amazing—not at all what I expected," answered Olivia.

Justin laughed. "First-time visitors are always shocked at how small this place is. Come on, we have some time before we have to start helping out. Let's explore the old post office."

Olivia felt like she was slipping back in time as she stepped onto the wooden planks of the porch outside of the small, wood frame post office and general store. She imagined a couple of cowboys leaning up against the wall on the old wooden benches and sharing stories or taking a nap as a spring rain provided a constant patter on the tin roof.

Inside the store, the vintage oak teller window and the original post office boxes indicated the tiny post office had served only a small number of locals. Like many contemporary general stores in tourist towns, old antique glass cases were full of handcrafted jewelry of all types, some designed by local artists. Ball hats and tee shirts of all sizes, colors, and designs lined the shelves and hung from the ceiling. On both sides of the tiny aisle were racks and shelves full of a combination of old-fashioned relics and modern day trinkets and souvenirs. Above the shelves, hung a variety of western paintings.

"Look," said Justin. "That's one of my Aunt Beth's paintings. She's a well-known western artist," he bragged. "She donated one of her paintings to be auctioned off today during the first break of the concert."

Olivia moved closer to get a better look at the painting. "It's so detailed and realistic," she said. "It almost looks like a photograph."

"She's amazing, all right. I wish I had some of her talent. Come on, I want to show you the old tavern attached to the back of the store."

"Wait, I've got to have one of those shirts," she said, pointing to a pink tee with the famous phrase *Everybody is somebody in Luchenbach* printed across the back.

"I've got lots of those shirts," said Justin. "I'll give you one."

"I bet you don't have a pink one," responded Olivia.

"You've got that right. Go ahead, and I'll just wait for you outside on the patio next to the bar."

Olivia made her purchase and then headed out the back of the store through the small bar where all sorts of beverages including the popular Texas ale, *Shiner Bock*, were sold. On one side of the bar was a small serving window that overlooked the spacious outdoor eating area that was entirely shaded by another giant oak tree. Rows of long wooden tables and benches signaled this was a place to meet and enjoy the company of strangers from all over.

The remnants of the old cotton gin that once was a vital part of the economy of the town now served as a small outdoor stage and public restrooms. Old automobile license plates were nailed over holes in the wood on buildings and along the wooden walkways and fence rails.

Olivia quickly spotted Justin, who was leaning against the wooden rail overlooking the creek below. "Don't you just love this place, Justin," she said. "Do you come here often?"

"Yeah, I do. There's always great Texas music here all the time, and there's plenty of opportunity to meet all types of people from all over."

Olivia chuckled as she noticed the population figures of Luchenbach painted on a guitar near one of the large oak trees. Black letters on the red, white, and blue guitar read: Population: 03. "Well, according to that sign, there aren't too many residents here."

"No, there aren't many full-time residents, but there are always tourists from everywhere milling around the town."

"I've read about the concerts Willie Nelson held here," said Olivia.

"The song, *Luchenbach Texas*, he and Whalen Jennings recorded immortalized the town and has made it the center of Texas country music. Lots of stars got their start here, even Jan."

"Really? I didn't know that about her, and I thought I knew everything ever published about her."

"Speaking of her, we'd better head over to the temporary stage they've set up in the middle of the field out there."

"I thought she'd be performing in the dance hall," said Olivia.

"The dance hall can't hold the crowd the big concerts bring in. And from the looks of that line of traffic, this one's bringing in a lot of them. The music will be broadcast

100

inside of the dance hall and all over the place, but most people will gather around the stage."

"This is my first concert," said Olivia.

"You're kidding, right?"

"No, I've never been to a big concert, ever," responded Olivia. "I've seen a few performers who sang a song or two at the rodeos, but I've never been to a real, live concert."

"Well, believe me, you're in for a real experience. There's nothing like a live concert. My Aunt Jan is a dynamite performer. Of course, there won't be all the lights at this one since it's outside during the day, but she can really stir up an audience. Let's go." He grabbed hold of Olivia's hand, and they jogged toward the large tent and outdoor stage in the middle of the field.

"Howdy you two," called Jan as they ducked inside the white tent set up as a temporary dressing room for Jan and the other musicians. "What do you think of Luchenbach, Olivia? Isn't it great?"

"I have to admit I was shocked at first, but I love it."

Olivia could hardly believe what she was experiencing. She was actually standing in the dressing room of her favorite country-western singer, something she would never have dreamed was possible. *This is all surreal*, she thought. *I can't believe this is actually happening to me.* She glanced over at Jan. She was undoubtedly the most beautiful person Olivia had ever known. Everything about her was perfect—

her hair, her smooth skin, her sparkling, green eyes, and her perfect figure. *She has it all,* mused Olivia. *And on top of that, she's perfectly humble and unspoiled by her success.*

She admired the outfit Jan was wearing. The simple and chic ankle length, mustard-colored skirt was made of a soft denim fabric and was split in front up to the knee exposing her shapely, tanned legs and her cream-colored boots. The metallic foil print of her smooth fitting, sleeveless blouse was swirled with the same shades of mustard and cream to match her skirt and boots. The collar of the blouse was studded with tiny crystals that created sparkles of light under Jan's chin. Around her waist, she wore a large, crystal-studded belt attached to one of the many silver buckles she had won with Raven. Her auburn hair was pulled to the side, and a fresh gardenia was tastefully nestled in the center of a French knot. Around her neck was a large, rhinestone cross—something she wore at every concert. According to the magazine articles Olivia had read about Jan, the cross was a gift from her dad, who was killed in the same air crash that killed Justin's father.

"Okay, folks," called Roger as he entered the tent. "It's show time. Nice outfit, Jan. Your wardrobe designer certainly has good taste." He smiled and winked at Jan, knowing full-well that he always had the final say in her show outfits and that he had picked out what she was wearing today.

"Come on, Olivia," called Justin. "Let's head to our post on the ground in front of the stage. We have to help prevent people from climbing on the stage and trying to grab a piece of Aunt Jan."

"Do people actually do that?" asked Olivia.

"You'll be surprised. Here," he said, handing her a two-way radio and an ear piece. "Just call me if anyone gives you a rough time."

"Good grief," muttered Olivia. "Why would someone do that?"

Justin laughed and led her to her position in front of the stage.

The crowd went crazy when the band began playing Jan's theme song, *A Cowgirl's Dream*. Even outside in the wide open fields, the noise from the enormous crowd was deafening as the audience hooted, whistled, and clapped when Jan walked out onto the stage. Olivia turned around to glance up at Jan, and immediately a fan tried to shove past her to climb onto the stage. "Get back," she shouted to the young man. "Let her sing, and you just enjoy the music for Pete's sake." She grabbed him by his shirt and pulled him away from the stage. Justin rushed over to help hold him down until two uniformed officers escorted the unruly fan away.

"Are you okay?" Justin shouted to Olivia.

"Yeah, but I had no idea there were nuts like that around. Entertaining is not all glamour and glory is it?"

"Not by a long shot," answered Justin. "There's always at least one jerk in every crowd that tries to grab some piece of her. Hopefully, he's the only one today. The more famous she gets, the less privacy she has, and the more security she needs. Roger and Brett make sure that she has constant security, but she can't go anywhere off the ranch without a disguise. She really is sort of a prisoner of her own fame."

Olivia turned and glanced up at the stage. She had no idea that Jan had to give up so much to share her talent with others. "It shouldn't be like that," she muttered.

Between Jan's sessions, local musicians and other young stars entertained the crowd. It was almost dusk when Jan came on stage for her signature closing song, *Keep Your Eyes on Heaven*. A hush fell over the entire crowd when she asked for a moment of silence for the families who had lost their homes and their loved ones during the tornado. Tears streamed down Olivia's cheeks as she realized how lucky she had been on that terrible day. Although she had tried several times to find the small cavern that had protected her and Bud from the storm, she had never been able to find it again. "Thank you," she said looking up to the sky.

Chapter 14

Olivia galloped Bud across the dusty flatland on her way home from the Triple Bar. She was excited because today was the first time she would attempt to ride Sonny. They had put the saddle and bridle on him at the start of the week. He hadn't paid much attention to the saddle but fought hard against opening his mouth and accepting the bit. He didn't, however, rear or try to run away from them—a positive sign he had learned to trust them. But he absolutely refused to open his mouth to let them slip in the bit until Olivia carefully stuck her thumb into his mouth behind the ridge of his back teeth. She gently massaged his back gums and gradually applied a little pressure on them. With a little verbal encouragement, Sonny finally opened his mouth. Tom quickly slipped in a piece of peppermint, and Olivia removed the pressure on his gums.

After several days of this process, Sonny began to open his mouth immediately when Olivia touched it. Yesterday, instead of the peppermint, Tom gently slid a bit lightly covered with honey into his mouth. Sonny played with the bit for a while, and then they let him spit it out. Today, they intended to slip the bridle over his ears, and he wouldn't be able to spit out the pesky bit.

"Good morning, honey," called Tom from the paddock as Olivia hopped down from Bud.

Olivia noticed Sonny was already saddled but was not sporting the bridle. Her dad was warming him up by walking him around the paddock on a lead line. Tom's crutches were laying on the ground next to the gate. He didn't need them as much now that he had a walking cast on his leg.

"Hi, Dad," she called. "Just give me a few minutes to cool Bud down and brush him, and then I'll help you bridle Sonny."

"No hurry, darlin'. Sonny and I are just getting our morning exercise."

Olivia unsaddled Bud and led him into the paddock to walk him and cool him down after their mad dash from the Triple Bar. As she caught up with her dad, Sonny softly nickered as if he were welcoming them. Olivia slowly reached over and lightly touched his nose, and he gently sniffed her hand. "I'm so excited about getting a chance to climb on Sonny and see what he does that I can hardly stand it," she said.

"I don't think he'll do much," replied Tom. "He hardly paid any attention when you leaned across the saddle the other day or when we put the sand bags onto the saddle yesterday. He's had people on his back at the other trainers. It's getting him to accept the bit that's going to be our challenge."

"You can't really blame him for not wanting that cold, hard piece of metal in his mouth," defended Olivia. "How would you like to have something clanging around on your back teeth or pulling on the sides of your mouth and pushing against your tongue and the roof of your mouth."

"It's our job to make sure everything lays and fits right so nothing pinches him or bumps up against his teeth. But he has to feel the pressure if we're going to get him to respond and move the way we want him to."

"I know, but I wish I could just grab hold of his mane and let him race his race."

"You could do that, but you'd better be ready to go where he wants to go and to stop when he feels like stopping."

"Probably not too practical when I'm racing him," she replied. She glanced over at her dad to see how the suggestion of her being Sonny's full-time jockey was accepted.

Tom turned toward her and stared at her for a moment. "Who said you'd be racing with him? I don't mind you exercising him, but I still don't want you on his back in a race."

"Well, let's not argue about it now. We'll just see how it all plays out." She smiled as she realized that her dad's tone had softened a little. At least he hadn't voiced his objection to her racing Sonny as vehemently as he had several weeks ago. "I'm going to take Bud back to the barn. It'll only take me a few minutes to brush him down and feed him. I'll bring Sonny's bridle back with me."

"It's hanging on the fence post over there," replied Tom pointing to the gate.

When she returned to the paddock, Olivia grabbed the bridle

and headed toward her dad and Sonny. "Are you ready for this, little fellow," she asked lightly stroking Sonny on the neck and holding the bridle up for him to see it.

"Here, give it to me," replied Tom. He took hold of the bit and held it in his hands for a minute to make sure it was at body temperature. Next he rubbed an unwrapped peppermint over the bit and then let Sonny have the candy before he tried to put the bit in his mouth. After Sonny was finished with the peppermint, Tom gently put pressure on the top of Sonny's head until he dropped it. Immediately, he held the bit against Sonny's mouth while he simultaneously slipped his left thumb behind Sonny's back teeth, slowly putting pressure on his back gums. Sonny tossed his head to the side just once and then finally opened his mouth and took the bit. Tom quickly slipped the bridle over Sonny's ears. "Thanks, fellow. That wasn't so bad was it?" he said softly.

"Halleluiah," whispered Olivia.

Tom gently pulled the side of Sonny's mouth back to make sure the bit was seated properly and wasn't pressing against his back teeth or pinching his tongue. "Okay, darlin'," he said, turning toward Olivia. "Are you ready for this?"

"I was born ready for this," bragged Olivia.

Tom pulled lightly on the reins to get Sonny to turn his head, so he could see it was Olivia who was about to climb on his back. He then gave Olivia a leg up, and she lowered herself slowly into the saddle.

"Easy, Sonny," she whispered. "This is exciting for both of us; I know."

Tom handed her the reins and stepped back. "Be ready, honey. He's arching his back a little."

"I can feel it," said Olivia calmly. "I'm just going to let him stand here for a minute and see what he'll do."

"Don't let him lower his head if you don't want him to send you to the moon," warned Tom.

"Dad," said Olivia, "this is not the first time I've ridden an unbroken horse for goodness sake. Just relax, will you? You're acting the same way you did the first time you ever put me on a horse. I've got this."

Sonny suddenly lunged forward and darted around the paddock, kicking and throwing his rear legs out, but he didn't actually try to throw her off. "Yippee," shouted Olivia. "I knew he'd have spunk."

"You'd better get him under control," shouted Tom.

"Leave us alone. I want him to play a little and let him know I'm not going anywhere."

Tom sighed and turned his back. He couldn't bear to watch the two wild things racing around the paddock. After several minutes, Sonny stopped his kicking and bucking, and Olivia reached out to pat him on the neck. "That was fun," she shouted to her dad.

"Not for me," replied Tom.

Olivia laughed and continued to walk Sonny around the paddock working with him to get him used to responding to her leg pressure on his sides and to her simultaneous voice commands as she started and stopped him. "Look how responsive he is, Dad."

"Yeah, he obviously knows what to do, but those other idiots who had him first never took the time to build up his confidence before they started jerking him around."

"That's what makes you a super trainer, Dad. Look at how well I turned out."

"Yeah, you're okay, I guess—a little wild and stubborn, but aside from that, you've turned out to be a fine, young filly."

"And I'm the perfect partner for Sonny. You have to be able to see that now."

"You never give up, do you?" He sighed and turned around heading back toward the barn.

"And I never will," she called after him.

Chapter 15

Tom sat down at the kitchen table and opened the logbook of his proposed race schedule for Sonny. He wanted to check the plan one more time before Brett arrived at the cabin to go over it with him. His plan included taking Sonny to Ruidoso early, so he could get experience racing against other horses in the schooling races. He had also scheduled plenty of rest between the schooling races and the other futurity races before the All American trials in August.

"Hey, Tom," called Brett through the screen door.

"Come on in, Brett."

"Coffee sure smells good," said Brett inhaling a long, deep breath.

"Help yourself. I just made a fresh pot. There're some warm biscuits and honey over there if you'd like some."

Brett pulled a huge mug off the shelf above the kitchen sink and filled it with coffee. He grabbed two large biscuits and a huge dollop of honey and returned to the table where Tom had spread out Sonny's race schedule. "Jan and I have both become addicted to Olivia's biscuits."

"She knows how to make a light, flaky biscuit, that's for sure."

"Speaking of Olivia, where is she?" asked Brett. "Isn't she

going to be part of this discussion?"

Tom took a long sip of coffee before answering. "She's upstairs in bed. She usually plops into bed about this time every morning. She's pretty tired by the time she helps out at the Triple Bar all night and then comes over here to work with Sonny. But to be honest, I intentionally didn't tell her that you were coming over this morning."

Brett spread the honey over one of the biscuits and gazed up at Tom. "Really? Why not?"

"I wanted to talk to you first. You know she's got her mind made up that she's going to jockey Sonny."

"Do you have a problem with that?" asked Brett licking the honey from his fingers.

Tom hesitated for a moment before answering. "I..uh..I'm not actually sure how I feel about it. I know she can ride him; she's proved that. And I know that he trusts her and would run his heart out for her."

"So, what you're really worrying about is her, right?"

"I know how dangerous racing is. I've seen a lot of jockeys hurt bad. I would hate like hell to have something happen to her. And besides that, I wasn't sure how you'd feel about starting out with a woman as your jockey."

Brett laughed. "Well, since we're being honest here—at first, I was against it—for the same reason you are and because I really didn't think she could hold her own

116

against the other, more experienced jockeys. But then I mentioned my concerns to Jan, and she about ripped my head off for being, and I quote, *a typical chauvinistic, male obstructionist to the abilities and gifts that women bring to the horse industry.* Then, in typical female retaliation, she banned me to the couch until I reconsidered."

Tom smiled. "I heard the same sentiment from Olivia but a little less eloquently expressed and followed by the silent treatment. But I still can't get past the risk of her getting hurt."

"I can appreciate that, Tom, but I think if you don't give her the chance to make her own decision, you're taking an even greater risk of losing her in another way."

Tom was silent for several minutes and then finally muttered, "Man, I hate these decisions, but I know you're right. Maybe after the first few smaller races, she'll decide on her own that she can't handle it."

"Don't count on it," said Brett. "She's a lot like Jan, and once she decides to do something, she'll give it all she's got to get it done."

"Yes," whispered Olivia as she silently headed back up the stairway where she had been secretly eavesdropping on the conversation in the kitchen. *Now all I have to do is tell Justin that I'll be leaving in a few weeks*, she thought. Her initial joy at her dad's decision to let her race diminished a little as she thought about how Justin would react to her decision. She knew he was counting on her to show the gray mare this spring, but she finally realized that what she wanted more than anything was to fly into the Winner's Circle on Sonny. *He'll understand*, she decided as she slid under the smooth, soft sheets and put a pillow over her head to block out the sun that was streaming in through the lacey curtains that she had actually begun to appreciate.

Chapter 16

Olivia slowly pushed the porch swing back and forth as she waited for Justin to arrive for their nightly ride to the Triple Bar. The hot, sultry twilight hadn't cooled down much, even after the sun had finally turned its daily watch over to the moon. The slight breeze created by the swing brought little relief from the muggy night air. "Man, it's still as hot as July tonight," she groaned. The heat was unusual for this time of the year, and it hadn't rained since the day the tornado dumped huge piles of hail that quickly melted as they hit the parched, rock-hard ground. High heat and low precipitation records confirmed the ranchers' fear of the predicted summer drought.

Glancing out toward the paddock, she watched as Sonny and Nanny shared a long, cool drink from the huge, steel water tub. She whistled softly, and the two animals looked up and turned toward the porch. Sonny's ears strained forward to listen to the sound of her whistling.

The moonlight bounced off his shiny blackness and illuminated his strong, muscular body. Their daily exercise regimen and her dad's careful attention to Sonny's dietary needs had turned him into a statuesque model of equine perfection. He looked like one of those elegant statues that had so impressed her at the Kentucky Horse Park when she and her dad had visited there years ago. *He's such an incredible animal,* she mused. *He most certainly has in him the prowess and instinct it takes to be a winner. I just hope I don't hinder his potential for greatness with my own selfish desire to be the one on his back when he flies across the finish line ahead of all contenders.* She whistled again, and Sonny responded with a soft whinny. *It's like the two of us were meant to find one another,* she thought. We both have a wild side and a bullish desire to do things our way. I just hope we can do our thing together without causing either of us or anyone else to suffer any brutal consequences from our relentless pigheadedness.

She was so deep into her own thoughts that she hadn't noticed Justin's approach until he stepped out of the darkness onto the porch. "Oh, Justin, you scared me," she said, clutching her chest. When she looked up at him, she knew immediately he had already heard the news about her decision to jockey Sonny. Her heart sank when she recognized the coolness and disappointment in his eyes.

"You looked like you were lost in some pretty deep thought," said Justin as he plopped down in the swing next to her. "I wasn't sure whether you wanted to come over to the Triple Bar tonight, but I decided to come by just in case," he muttered, without looking at her.

"Of course I want to come with you. Why wouldn't I?"

Justin turned and stared at her for a few moments without answering her. Finally, he responded, "Well, then, I guess we should get going." He immediately got up and headed toward the porch steps.

"Justin, please tell me that you support my decision to race Sonny."

He hesitated on the first step and then slowly turned around to look at her. "Sorry, Olivia, I can't tell you that."

"Why not?" she demanded.

"I'm not actually sure why I can't support your decision. I just know in my gut that it's not a good choice for you or for Sonny."

"Why? You don't think I can do it, do you?"

"Sometimes, Olivia, it's not about can or can't; it's about should or shouldn't."

"Why shouldn't I race Sonny then? You have to give me a reason. You just can't say something like that without an explanation."

"There's a lot more at stake here than you getting to feel the exhilaration of riding on top of a speeding horse."

"Don't you think I know that?"

"I'm not sure, do you? Have you really thought about how much Brett has at stake here? He's invested a lot of money in Sonny. And what about your dad? His future may depend on Sonny's success."

"I'm not naïve, Justin. I know that they both have a lot to lose if Sonny and I don't win."

"I'm not through, Olivia. What about Sonny? It's obvious that he has the speed and athleticism to be a Super Horse, but it isn't all up to him. He needs someone on his back who knows how to maneuver him through the pack. You've never ridden in any major race, have you? So, how could you possibly know the strategies of racing?"

"My dad will teach me. He knows everything about racing, and I can learn."

"Fine." He shook his head and stared out into space. For several minutes, neither of them said anything.

Olivia struggled to hold back the bitter tears that burned her eyes. She was hurt and disappointed. She had been so certain that Justin would understand her decision, but obviously, he didn't.

Heaving a long sigh, Justin softly whispered, "If you do this, you'll be gone all the time. What about us, Olivia?"

"What do you mean?"

He stared at her for a moment then slowly shook his head, dropping his chin to his chest. Finally, he softly muttered, "Well, if you have to ask what I mean, I guess it isn't really an issue." Abruptly, he whirled around and stomped down the stairs. "If you're coming with me, come on. We have a lot of horses to ride tonight, and I have to decide which of them to take with me this weekend. Our show season has already started, and we're behind our last year's schedule because I wanted to give you more time with the gray mare."

Olivia sat frozen in the swing. She felt a heaviness that

she had never felt before. Earlier this morning, when she learned that she was to have the chance to race Sonny, she felt like a free-floating balloon soaring to greater and greater heights, but now she felt as if the balloon had suddenly popped, and she was swirling and plummeting out of control. She was paralyzed and unable to think or move from the swing. Justin's obvious lack of confidence in her stunned and hurt her deeply.

"Are you coming?" he asked as he leaned down from his horse to untie Bud's reins from the porch railing.

She stared at him for several moments. "No, Justin. I guess I won't be coming over to the Triple Bar any more. I'm sorry if I've compromised your show schedule. I didn't mean to have things end this way." She watched as Justin slowly looped Bud's reins back around the porch railing, and then, without looking at her, he spurred his horse into a gallop and flew across the yard without uttering a word.

She continued to stare at the cloud of dust as he disappeared beyond the paddock. After what seemed like hours, she finally pushed herself up from the porch swing and headed down the steps to lead Bud back to the barn. As she passed by his paddock, Sonny stretched his neck over the railing and gently nudged her shoulder with his soft muzzle. "Thanks, fellow," she said turning to wrap her arms around his graceful neck. "We can do this, can't we?" Sonny tilted his head upward and blasted his strongest whinny. In the distance, she heard Raven echo his call. "Well, then, tomorrow we tackle the problem of getting you used to the starting gate, my dear friend. We're going to show them all," she proclaimed.

Chapter 17

The next morning, Olivia slowly dragged herself down the stairs and into the kitchen at 5:00. She had tossed and turned all night, unable to clear her mind of the painful look she had seen in Justin's eyes when she had purposely avoided answering his comment about their relationship and about her leaving for the summer.

Tom glanced up from the griddle as he expertly flipped over a pancake. "Wow, you must have finished early at the Triple Bar. I didn't even hear you come in this morning."

Olivia plopped into her chair at the table. Even though she had her back to him, she could still feel the scrutinizing gaze from her dad. She didn't dare to turn around to look at him because she knew that somehow he could always see right through to her soul. "I didn't go to the Triple Bar last night," she said trying to sound light-hearted. "I won't be going over there anymore because I've decided to concentrate on getting Sonny ready for his first race."

"Lover's quarrel?" asked her dad. He placed a high stack of pancakes on the table in front of Olivia.

"Lover's quarrel? I have no idea what you're talking about."

Tom shook his head and walked back to get the butter and syrup for the pancakes. "You don't, huh?" He paused and sighed. "Then that's too bad," he muttered.

Olivia reached out and slid a pancake onto her plate without looking at him. "Dad, come on. Justin and I are not lovers, for heaven's sake. He only puts up with me because Jan told him to."

Tom sat down next to his daughter and lightly touched her wrist. "Whoa! Are you totally blind or are you just so wrapped up in yourself and Sonny that you've stopped paying attention to the rest of us? Where has my sensitive, caring daughter disappeared to?" he said lightly shaking her arm.

"What *are* you talking about?" Olivia responded angrily yanking her arm away from him.

"You know darn good and well what I'm talking about. You used to be sensitive to the needs of everyone around you. Now it's as if you don't care about anyone or anything except that horse and your goal of riding him in the Futurity. There's a heck of a lot more to life than becoming the best female jockey or taming the wildest horse, Olivia. You'd better learn that and learn it fast, or someday you'll end up like me—worn out and alone."

"Good grief, Dad. I'm only twenty. I have a right to live my life before I have to make long-lasting choices. I care for Justin. I care a lot for him. I may even love him. I don't know. I haven't really had much chance to know what that feels like."

Tom stabbed at a huge bite of pancakes with his fork, but halfway to his mouth, he lowered the fork back to the plate. He leaned across the table at Olivia. "I wasn't suggesting that you get married, for Pete's sake. I was just saying you need to be sensitive about how he feels about you. I doubt if he's ready for marriage either, for that matter, but it's obvious that he cares deeply for you. You seem to be blind about the way he looks at you. I've watched you. You don't even notice his looks."

"You're wrong. That's not true. I like the way he looks at me. It gives me a warm feeling deep in the pit of my stomach—a feeling that I've never felt before—and I miss him when I'm not with him. But I don't know what to say or do when he looks at me that way. I just don't know how to act or feel. Besides, isn't he supposed to make the first move?"

Tom tried unsuccessfully to avoid laughing aloud, but he couldn't control himself. He suddenly burst into hysterical laughter spraying his mouthful of pancakes across the table.

"Stop it," shouted Olivia shoving her chair back from the table and darting for the stairs.

"I'm sorry," muttered Tom trying desperately to regain control of himself. "Come back here, young lady. I wasn't laughing at you. I was just laughing because I knew someday this moment would come, and I've always been afraid that I wouldn't know how to handle it. Obviously, I was right. I don't know how to handle it."

"You sure don't," agreed Olivia, plopping back down in her chair. "So can we talk about something you do know how to handle—like how to get Sonny used to the starting gate."

"Okay, I'm sorry. I shouldn't have pried into something that I don't know how to help you with. But before we leave the topic, I think you should make an effort to see Justin one more time before we leave. Men don't have to make the 'first move'—not anymore. As a matter of fact, they've always hated having to make the first move. They're just as afraid as you are of being rejected. It's actually a wonder that men and women ever get together. Animals are just so much smarter than we are about such things. With them, it's easy—a simple mating ritual, and the whole thing is settled."

"Dad, please. Pass me the pancakes, and let's change the subject."

"Fine, but at least promise me that you'll try to see Justin before we leave."

"OK, OK. Now let's talk about Sonny and the starting gate. I'm a little worried about that. He doesn't seem to like tight spaces. I learned that when I tried to lead him into that small gap in the rocks during the tornado."

"No horses like tight places; they're claustrophobic by nature, so I'm counting on Nanny and Bud to help us out with this one. They should be able to keep Sonny calm until he gets used to the gate. It's always an uncomfortable place for a horse, and his natural instinct is to resist going in. When he's finally forced to enter the gate, and he feels it close behind him, he's likely to panic. He feels trapped, and all he wants to do is to get out of there. He can easily hurt himself and you by rearing inside that small space, so you always have to watch yourself. If he feels your nervousness, he becomes even more anxious, so you have to stay calm and try to reassure him. You'll be able to tell when he's about to rear or bolt if you just keep focused on the tension that's building in him. Some gates have narrow alleys between the stalls, but many of them don't, so there's no place for you to go in that confined place except to jump onto the rails, but even that's dangerous. If you fall inside the gate, you'll likely be trampled or crushed before the starting gate loaders can open the gate and get to you."

Olivia listened closely to her dad. She could see in his eyes and hear in his voice the fear that he obviously had for her safety, but she wasn't afraid. She was ready, and she knew that Sonny had learned to trust her. This morning would show just how much that trust would be able to overcome his natural instincts.

"We'd better get out there," said Tom interrupting her thoughts. "The sun is going to be up pretty soon, and the heat will just add to Sonny's stress level."

"I'm ready," said Olivia shoving the last bite of pancakes into her mouth. She grabbed her plate and her dad's and headed for the sink.

"Just leave the dishes for later," said Tom. "Let's get this day over with."

As they walked out the door together, Olivia linked her arm through her dad's. "I can do this, Dad. I know I can."

Tom stopped at the bottom of the porch steps and turned

to stare into his daughter's excited, blue eyes. "I know you can, sweetie. I know you can. I just don't know if I can stand to watch it."

Chapter 18

For two days, they tried unsuccessfully to load Sonny into the small schooling gate. By the third day, Olivia was losing patience with the whole process. "Please, Sonny," she begged. "I promise there's nothing that will hurt you inside that gate. Look at Bud and Nanny. They're not afraid. They're just standing in there munching away on that delicious alfalfa. Wouldn't you like to join them for breakfast?"

"He's thinking about it, Olivia. Just walk him around the gate one more time and let him relax. I think he'll go in today. I just feel it," called Tom from his perch on the railing along the track.

"We've been at this for two solid days, and he hasn't once gotten within three feet of the gate," groaned Olivia. "Maybe I should try riding him in instead of just leading him in from the ground."

"No. He has to be able to do it from the ground before I'll let you try riding him in," shouted Tom. "Try it again. He looked a little less hesitant the last time."

Everything her dad did with Sonny was first accomplished on the ground without a rider. Olivia realized that it was important to teach the horse on the ground first to reduce the risk of injury to the horse and its rider, but she was getting frustrated and tired of Sonny's stubbornness. "Come on, fellow. Don't be a wimp. March in there like the stud you are," she pleaded.

She led him once more around the outside of the starting gate letting him stop to greet Bud nose-to-nose. Bud looked up from his morning treat and whinnied softly. "See, Bud likes it in there. Please, Sonny, just go into the stall next to Bud and get your morning treat. You'll be fine, I promise," she urged. As they approached the back of the gate, she watched him closely. Maybe her dad was right. Sonny appeared to be more relaxed this morning. He hadn't shied away from the gate like he did yesterday and the day before. But as they approached the open stall next to Bud, Sonny planted his front feet in the ground and then sped backward away from the gate, dragging her with him. "Darn it, Sonny. This is ridiculous," she shouted.

"Try it again," called Tom calmly. "Just back him up a few steps then lead him straight through the gate. I keep telling you that you're hesitating right before you go in. Don't stop."

"It all must seem pretty simple when you're just perched over there on the fence rail," Olivia responded sarcastically. She heaved a big sigh, pushed Sonny backward several steps, and then quickly walked him up to the gate once more without breaking her stride. To her surprise, Sonny followed her right through the enclosure and out the front gate with no problem. "Halleluiah," she shouted and quickly rewarded him with a peppermint and a hug around his neck. "Now that wasn't so hard, was it?" she soothed.

"Not when he feels your confidence. Try it again, Olivia," shouted Tom.

Olivia led him through the gate four more times without any difficulty. "Now can I get on and ride him in?" she called to her dad.

"Not yet," answered Tom, sliding down from the fence. "We've got to see what happens when we close the gates on him. Lead him through one more time and then make him stand there while you step out. When I say so, I want you to push the front gate closed with you on the outside. Then walk away, and I'll shut the back gate. If he rears, stay clear until I open my gate, so he can back out."

Once again, Olivia led Sonny around the perimeter of the gate and then headed into the stall next to Bud. Sonny walked in behind her without faltering. "Here, big guy," she said as she handed him a handful of hay that she pulled from Bud's hay bag. "Just stand there and enjoy the snack," she encouraged as she backed slowly out of the gate.

"Good," said Tom. "Now close the front gate."

Cautiously, Olivia grabbed hold of the front gate and slowly began to close it. The metal hinges on the gate screeched, and Sonny's eyes darted toward the sound. "Easy, Sonny," she assured. "I'm not going anywhere."

"Okay, now move over in front of Bud's stall, and watch yourself if Sonny starts to rear," warned Tom. "A panicked horse will strike out with his front legs and can wallop a fatal blow to your head if you're not careful."

"I know, Dad. I wasn't born yesterday. Just close the gate, will ya?"

"We don't want to hurry this. Show some patience, for heaven's sake," said Tom as he began slowly to close the rear gate. At the sound of a noise behind him, Sonny immediately backed up, crashing hard against the rear railing and shaking the entire starting gate.

Nanny looked up from her pile of hay and bleated as if to tell him to settle down. Bud turned toward Sonny's stall and nickered softly. For a few seconds, Sonny continued to lunge forward and backward, banging against the front and back rails, until he finally settled down. He then grabbed a mouthful of hay from Bud's hay bag and just stood there looking around.

"Way to go, Sonny," whispered Olivia reaching over the gate to pat him on the head. "You did it."

"Okay, I'm going to open the rear gate and let him back out. I don't want him to come out the front gate yet."

"Why not?"

"I want him to understand that when that front gate opens, he has to fly out of there in a straight line, alert and ready to race at top speed. He'll learn that easier with you on his back. That's enough for today. Tomorrow it's your turn to show what you can do with him."

"We've still got some time before it gets too hot. Can't we try it today?" Olivia begged.

"Nope, that's it for today. You always end a horses' training on a high note. Once they've responded the way you want them to, you reward them by stopping the training. You can saddle him up and jog him around the track a little before you put him away if you feel like it but don't overdo it. The sun is already starting to burn a hole straight through my hat to my brain. Besides, I told Brett that I'd come up to the main house this morning to make the final arrangements for leaving this weekend. Don't do anything stupid with that horse while I'm gone."

"We're leaving this weekend?" called Olivia.

"Yes, you knew that; so that leaves you only two days to keep your promise about going to see Justin."

"Do I have to?" she shouted.

"Get it done, Olivia. I mean it."

"But I don't see what good that's going to do," she shouted, kicking the ground with her boot and sending a cloud of dust flying through the air toward her father.

"Just do it, Olivia," he replied.

She was still seething when she rode out of the barn and headed toward the track to give Sonny a light workout. As she rode past the starting gate, she suddenly pulled him to a stop. "I don't see why we can't take a few runs out of the starting gate this morning," she said aloud. She leaned over to pat Sonny on the neck. "No one needs to know we did it, and we'll look better tomorrow if we practice a little today."

Slowly, she inched Sonny toward the rear of the starting gate. She could feel his nervousness as he pranced sideways a few steps before heading straight through the narrow gate. "Easy, Sonny, we can do this, big fellow. I promise that everything will be all right," she whispered. She realized she was trying to assure herself as much as she was trying to calm Sonny. It was clear that Sonny was more hesitant about entering the gate with her on his back, but he responded to her cues to move forward until they were inside of the tight space. It seemed a lot smaller now than when she had simply walked through it. She pulled her knees in close to keep from banging them against the rails on both sides of her. "It's sort of close quarters in here, isn't it, buddy?" she whispered. Sonny continued to nervously prance around inside of the cramped space, but he made no attempt to rear or dart out of the open gate in front of him.

She continued to keep him standing inside the gate, waiting for him to settle down and relax a little more. As she leaned forward to rub him on the neck, out of nowhere, a hawk swooped down from the sky making a hideous, screeching sound as it flew past them. Sonny immediately catapulted out of the gate as if he had been shot out of a cannon. His sudden lunge jerked the reins out of Olivia's hands and sent her flying backward over his hindquarters and crashing to the ground behind him like a ton of bricks. For several moments, she was paralyzed with pains shooting every which way through her body. The fall knocked the wind out of her, and she was unable to breathe.

Strange thoughts flashed through her scrambled mind. *Breathe. I have to breathe. Oh, my god, I hurt everywhere.*

My dad is going to kill me when he comes back and finds Sonny gone and me sprawled out here on the ground. I can't just lay here until someone finds me. The sun is going to fry my brain; there's not one cloud in the sky. I need to wiggle my toes and fingers to see if I'm still all connected. She moved her fingers, and then she tried to move her feet. *Good—they still move. I must not have broken my neck or back, but boy it feels like I did.* "Okay," she muttered aloud. "I can't just lie here on the ground. I have to try to get up. On three, move. One, two, three. Ouch, ouch, ouch, I can't move. I can't."

She continued to lay there on the ground, trying to figure out what to do. "Maybe, if I roll over on my side, then I can inch over to the gate and grab hold of the rails to help myself up." She eventually got up the nerve to roll over to her left side. "Ouch, that hurt big time" she screamed. "Now what?" She reached out and grabbed the rail to pull herself up. "Oh, oh, that hurts."

Finally, she managed to sit up and lean against the gate. For several minutes, she just sat there and tried to get her breath. When the sound of approaching horses finally broke through to her consciousness, she looked down the track, hoping to see some trace of Sonny. In the distance, she could see a cloud of dust and what looked like two horses coming toward her. She grabbed hold of the railing again and, with considerable effort, struggled to her feet. She instantly felt light headed and for a moment thought she might actually vomit. Leaning over from the waist and bracing herself with her hands on her thighs, she drew in a deep breath hoping the nausea would go away.

When she looked back toward the approaching horses, she could plainly see Justin ponying Sonny. Thank goodness, there was no indication that Sonny had been injured in the mayhem.

"Are you okay?" shouted Justin jumping down from his horse and racing toward her.

"Sure," she lied. "What makes you think I wouldn't be fine?"

"Oh, I don't know, maybe it's that greenish color covering your face or the fact that you haven't attempted to move or let loose of that death grip you have on the gate. What happened?"

Olivia burst into tears. "My dad is going to kill me," she sobbed. "He told me not to do anything stupid, and I sure made a mess of everything."

Justin reached out and gently pulled her toward him. "Where do you hurt?" he asked pushing her dust-filled hair back from her face.

"Everywhere," she groaned. "I hurt everywhere."

"Do you think you can walk?"

"I'm not sure."

"Well, hold on to me, and let's see what still works."

Justin wrapped his arms around her waist and gently pried

her hand loose from the gate. "There you go," he said. "See you can walk after all. Why don't I help you get back up on Sonny, and I can lead you up to the house. You have a Jacuzzi up there, don't you? You'll feel much better if you climb into a tub of hot Epson salt water and let the Jacuzzi massage your sore spots."

When they finally reached the house, Justin gently lifted her down from Sonny and carried her onto the porch. "There you go," he said, gingerly lowering her to the ground. "Can you make it all right from here on your own? You still look a little green around the edges?"

"Justin, I'm sorry about the other night," she blurted out. "I just didn't know what to say. Surely, you know I'll miss you terribly while I'm gone. You have to know that you're important to me. I just have never felt like this before. I didn't recognize the feelings."

He stared at her for several moments then leaned over and gently kissed her. "I've never felt like this before either," he whispered pulling her into his arms.

"Ouch," she groaned. "Sorry—that wasn't very romantic, was it?"

Justin laughed. "Go on in and climb into the Jacuzzi. I'll put the horses away and come back to check on you. We have to get you back together before your dad gets here. If he sees you like this, you can pretty much kiss your career as a jockey goodbye."

"I know. I know. You're actually willing to help me and not

tell him about this?"

"What you tell him is between the two of you. I still think this jockey thing is a bad idea, but, as my Aunt Jan explained to me last night, you have a right to do whatever you want to. Just remember to hold on the next time."

"It all happened so fast. I just went flying off backward."

"I know. It has happened to me more than once," he called over his shoulder as he headed down the steps. "When a half ton of power thrusts forward, you'd better be ready, or you're going to be left behind with nothing but air for a saddle and a bone jarring trip to the ground."

Chapter 19

Jan was glad to be back home for a few days. Her tour was going well, but there was simply no place like the ranch for regenerating her spirit and energy. The past two weeks she had been exhausted and barely able to complete her rigorous performances. When she didn't have to visit a local radio station or attend a press conference, she had spent most of each day napping in the motor coach. In the past, she would have spent the time working on new songs or new arrangements for older ones.

Since the beginning of the road tour, she continued to have bouts of flu-like symptoms that seemed bent on destroying her typical, insatiable appetite for big, juicy steaks and king-size cuts of prime rib. Roger was so worried about her that he had insisted that Brett fly out to meet them in Branson, Missouri last week, even though she was scheduled to return home for a week after the Branson shows. The two men spent the entire time in Branson practically smothering her with special dinners and treats to get her to eat more. But every time she tried to eat, the nauseousness overwhelmed her.

Today, she was feeling much better and was looking forward to lunch with her sisters. She loved being with Lacey and Beth. The three of them were not only sisters— they were friends. It hadn't always been that way growing up, though. Jan was the youngest of the three, and in their earlier years, the other two either ignored her altogether or tried to dictate her every move and thought. To escape their constant mothering, she had spent most of her early years in the barn with her dad.

From the time she was able to walk, he had taken her to the barn to watch as he trained the horses. She had been on the back of a horse for as long as she could remember. Family pictures show her sitting bareback on giant stallions when she was barely able to sit alone. She was very close to her dad and missed him terribly. The death of her parents in that fatal air crash that also killed Lacey's husband was a shock to all of them, but the loss of her father was particularly devastating to Jan. He taught her everything she knew about horses and made sure she had learned at a young age to respect them for the magnificent animals they were. He constantly reminded her never to forget that they were first and foremost animals with deeply seated instincts that could never be denied. *Animals are animals first and pets second,* he used to say. *When cornered or frightened, they will respond first to their instincts, and all the training in the world will be forgotten in a heartbeat, so don't turn your back on them or expect them to respond rationally in a crisis. That's how people get hurt.*

After the death of her parents, Jan became much closer to her sisters. Although neither of them rode as well or knew as much about horses as she did, she began to appreciate their advice about other aspects of her life. Lacey was the one with practical advice on almost everything; whereas, Beth was the free spirit who never did anything practical and was always encouraging Jan to sprout her wings and do things her own way. It was Beth's advice that Jan valued in arranging her shows and her career and Lacey's that she followed in personal matters.

As she turned her car into the drive of the Triple Bar, she admired the timeless beauty of the sprawling ranch house where the three of them had grown up. Though she loved her new home with Brett at the Kendall Ranch, it was here, at the Triple Bar, where she felt that special bond that only a family homestead can provide. The flowers surrounding the terrace patio and pool were in full bloom despite the drought, and the warm spring breeze filled the air with their sweet perfume. She drew in a long, deep breath, inhaling their tantalizing scent that was enhanced by the fragrance of the bluebonnets and honeysuckle that lined the fencerow along the pastures. "Home, sweet home," she mumbled.

"Hey there," yelled Lacey as she carried a carved melon basket full of fresh fruit to the round umbrella table on the patio. "You're prompt as usual, but, of course, Sister Beth isn't. She called and said she had to run to Fredericksburg for something. Whatever she had to have, it couldn't wait until after lunch. She wouldn't tell me what it was. You know her, always full of surprises and mystique."

Jan smiled at Lacey's obvious frustration with free-spirited Beth. She leaned across the console of the front seat of her car and grabbed the bottle of wine. "I brought a bottle of white wine that I hope will complement your delicious lunch."

"Oh, good."

"Can I help you with anything?"

"Nope, I've got it all under control. Let's just sit out here, until Beth gets here. Help yourself to a dish of fresh fruit."

As she dipped out a serving of the fresh fruit into the delicate, antique stemware that she recognized as belonging to their great grandmother, Jan was relieved that the sensation of nausea that she anticipated didn't overwhelm her. She heaved a big sigh, grateful that her appetite seemed to be coming back. "This tastes delightful," she muttered. "Why is it that food always tastes better outside?"

"Beth told me that you hadn't been feeling well. It shows in your face. You look a little pale and thin."

"I've had the flu ever since I left home. I haven't been able to eat anything lately, without instantly feeling sick."

"Really? That's interesting," said Lacey smiling.

"Interesting? It's been horrible."

The blast from the horn on Beth's white Cadillac convertible interrupted their conversation. "Don't tell any secrets until I get up there," shouted Beth.

Jan and Lacey watched as Beth reached in the back seat and grabbed a small gift bag. She scrambled toward them with her walking cane moving so fast that it was hardly visible. When she finally reached them, she thrust the bag at Jan.

"Wow, this bag is gorgeous. Did you create this?" asked Jan. The bright, lime green cloth bag was exquisitely hand-painted with a picture of a magnificent sunset on one side and the words from the chorus of Jan's song, "Keep

Your Eyes On Heaven," written in elegant calligraphy on the other side.

"I'm glad you like it. It's the original one that was used as the prototype for others that Roger is having made," babbled Beth. "He thinks we can sell these at your next concert."

"It's simply beautiful, Beth. I love it."

"Look inside," Beth encouraged. She glanced over at Lacey and winked. "I had to go to Fredericksburg to get this." She giggled like a teenager giving a surprise package to her best friend.

"It better be good," said Lacey. "You're late as usual."

"I'm not that late. It's just lucky I didn't get a speeding ticket."

Jan reached inside and pulled out a box. She stared at the label, and completely confused, she glanced up at her two sisters.

Beth instantly burst into gales of laughter and Lacey shouted, "Good idea, Beth. One of your better ones, for sure."

"What's going on here?" asked Jan. "An instant pregnancy test kit? I don't get it. Are you trying to tell us that you're pregnant again?"

Both of her sisters burst out laughing. Trying to catch her

breath, Beth finally blurted out. "No, silly. I'm not pregnant, but I'll bet you the earnings from the sale of those bags that you are."

"Me?" shouted Jan. "I'm not pregnant; I can't be," she stammered.

"Come on, let's go up to the house and find out," said Lacey grabbing the kit and taking Jan by the hand. "Lunch can wait another fifteen minutes. I agree with Beth. You no more have the flu than I do."

"You two are nuts," protested Jan. "I just had an examination a week or so before I started the tour. I certainly wasn't pregnant then."

"That was almost six weeks ago," reminded Beth. "Come on. What will it hurt to try the test?"

Her two sisters dragged Jan into the house with Beth reading the instructions as they went. As her sisters stood outside of the bathroom laughing, Jan suddenly yelled, "Oh my god."

"I knew it; I knew it," shouted Beth. "As soon as Roger told me your symptoms, I knew it."

When Jan walked out of the bathroom, the three of them started jumping up and down and hugging one another as if they had just won the mega-million lottery. Then suddenly Jan stopped and burst into tears. "What if the test is wrong? Brett and I have tried for a year to get pregnant, and so far, we haven't been able to." She sank down into a chair and began to wail like a small child. "If this is one of your sick jokes, it certainly isn't a funny one, Beth Marie Livingston-Allen," she accused.

"Jan," shouted Beth. "Surely, you don't think I would play such a trick on you? Your tears are just another validation of your crazy emotional state. Face it, dear Sister, you're pregnant. Uh huh, uh huh," she sang, dancing around the room with Lacey.

"Oh, my god," said Jan. "I have to go tell Brett."

"Oh, no you don't," interrupted Lacey. "Not until you eat this delicious lunch I spent all morning fixing for you. And I think you'd better go see Dr. Henderson before you tell Brett. Just to make sure this silly test is right."

"Oh, Lacey," moaned Beth. "You're always so darned practical. It takes all the fun out of the moment when you double check everything in life."

"No, Beth," replied Jan. "This time I think Lacey's right. I know how much Brett wants a baby, and I wouldn't want to get his hopes up only to find out that this silly test was wrong. And don't you dare say anything to Roger or anyone else until I tell Brett. Roger is totally incapable of keeping any secrets."

"Oh, all right, then," pouted Beth.

"OK, we all agree. Mum's the word until Jan sees Dr. Henderson. Now come on, let's eat," said Lacey. "Beth, open up Jan's wine. The two of us might as well enjoy it. Sorry, Jan dear, you'll have to get used to all the things you

146

can no longer eat, drink, or do, but believe me, it'll all be worth it in the end."

"Do?" said Jan. "What do you mean there are things that I can't do?"

"Well, for starters, you'd better check with Dr. Henderson about riding," suggested Lacey.

"Riding? Oh no, if I can't ride this summer, Justin will kill me. Olivia has already backed out on him."

"I don't know what Dr. Henderson will say about your riding, but if it were me, I certainly wouldn't take the chance if I were in your shoes, especially with the risks you take on a horse," said Beth.

"Did that sound advice actually come out of your mouth, Beth dear? You're actually delving out some practical advice? It'll most certainly snow tomorrow," teased Lacey.

"Oh, no," moaned Jan. "Poor Justin."

Chapter 20

Jan stood back and admired the table setting she had arranged for the special dinner she planned for Brett. This morning Dr. Henderson confirmed the results of the pregnancy test and told her the baby should arrive in early December. He also agreed with Lacey about restricting her riding because of the risk of falling from a horse. However, since she was in such excellent physical condition and because riding was part of her daily routine when she was at the ranch, he explained that exercising a horse at a slow walk or leisurely trot would not hurt her or the baby. Jan had laughed and explained that neither a slow walk nor a leisurely trot were part of her regimen with horses.

After she told Brett tonight about the baby, she would have to break the news to Justin that she would be sitting out this show season. She sighed. She had never missed a World Show since she first began competing at five-years-old. She would miss the excitement of competition, but she was not going to do anything that would sacrifice the birth of this baby.

Luckily, she didn't have a road tour planned for fall, but she did have some out-of-state performances scheduled. Her summer concerts wouldn't be an issue, but her late fall ones would have to be canceled. She and Roger would have to decide what to do about them since contracts had already been signed. She was certain that the agreements included an escape clause under certain conditions, and her current situation would no doubt qualify as reason to cancel the contracts, but they would have to do it right away. She didn't want to cause any unnecessary hardships for concert promoters. "My life is never simple." She heaved a long sigh and glanced at her watch.

Grabbing her jacket, she headed toward the barn. The sun was slowly sinking over the ridge as she walked along the path, and she stopped to look up at the beautiful Texas sky, "Thank you," she whispered.

Raven was nervously prancing in his stall when she slid open the heavy door. "Good evening, my gallant sire," she said. "Here you go." She held out her hand, and he quickly sucked in the peppermint candy. "I have something very exciting to tell you tonight, Raven."

To her astonishment, Raven gently rubbed his forehead against her stomach. "No. You couldn't know about it. I know you're special, but, surely, you're not that smart." She laughed at herself as she opened the back door of his stall to start their evening stroll. Raven nickered softly and followed her out into the muggy evening. "I'm going to have a baby, Raven. Isn't it wonderful?" Raven came to an abrupt stop, lifted his head toward the sky, and whinnied louder than she had ever heard him before. In the distance, she heard Sonny answer Raven's call, and then, for several moments, a constant chain of whinnies seemed to bounce among the hills surrounding the ranch.

Could it be? she wondered. *Nah. I'm getting carried away, but still, I've never heard a succession of whinnies like that before.* At the end of the pasture, she stopped to watch the sun sinking quickly over the ridge. "I never get tired of watching the sunset with you, Raven. And just think, soon you'll be having a little one sitting up there on your back, clinging to your thick mane and watching the sunset with us. I can't wait," she whispered patting her stomach.

When she turned to head back to the barn, she was surprised to see Brett running toward her at breakneck speed. "Thank god," he called out. "I was afraid something had happened to you."

"Why did you think that?" she asked.

"Because the last time I heard Raven whinny like he did tonight, the two of you were being attacked by that cougar. I heard him from the road as I was turning into the drive. Then it sounded like a dozen horses echoed his call. Didn't you hear it?"

"I did. It was amazing wasn't it?"

"It scared the dickens out of me and everyone else. Justin immediately called me to see if there was something wrong. I promised to call him back as soon as I found you." He reached in his pocket and whipped out his phone to call Justin. "Hey, Justin, everything's fine over here," he said. "I know. It was weird. Anyway, nothing to worry about this time, but thanks for checking."

"See what a stir you caused with your loud announcement, Raven," said Jan reaching up to hug him around the neck. "Now you've let the whole world know my secret."

"What are you talking about? What secret?" asked Brett.

"Well, this wasn't the way I had planned to tell you, but I guess this is just as good a time as any," gushed Jan.

Brett stared at her for just a moment and then suddenly grabbed her and pulled her into his arms. "Are you going to say what I think you're going to say?" he asked gently pushing her back from him to stare into her twinkling eyes. "I've been secretly hoping that all your sickness was something more than the flu, but I was afraid to say anything. Are we really pregnant?" he shouted.

"Well, I don't know about you, but I am," she answered laughing.

Chapter 21

Justin, Jan, and Brett arrived at the cabin early Saturday morning to help Olivia and Tom pack everything into the new fifty-three foot trailer that Brett had purchased for them to haul Sonny, Bud, and Nanny around the country. The elegant living and horse quarters in the trailer were the most beautiful that Olivia had ever seen. It was like having a luxurious home and a fully outfitted stable on wheels.

The living quarters had all the amenities of a luxury apartment with a full kitchen, one and a half baths, two sleeping areas, and a huge entertainment room furnished with two luxurious, leather recliners, an oversized sofa, an electric fireplace, and a large HD screen TV above the mantel. Four slide outs provided additional space in the entertainment room, kitchen, and bedrooms. The rich wood paneling on the walls and the thick carpeting on the floor added warmth and elegance to the interior of the trailer. The mix of the smell of leather and wood provided a soothing aroma that tantalized the nose like the smell of a new car or a brand new house. With the possible exception of Jan's private tour bus, Olivia had never seen a more elegant trailer in her life.

Tom was naturally more excited about the luxury stalls for Sonny, Bud, and Nanny and the new diesel truck he would be driving to pull the rig. Each of the three horse stalls had thick, soft padding on both sides and some sort of special spray-on flooring to prevent the animals from slipping. Along the interior of the stall area, small L.E.D. strips provided continuous, soft lighting. Each animal had a separate manger and a small fan to keep them comfortable on the road. What Tom appreciated most was the video camera that let him monitor the horses from the truck during travel.

"Oh, Justin," gushed Olivia. "Have you ever seen anything more luxurious in your life? I feel as if I've died and gone to heaven."

Justin tossed the last bale of alfalfa into the storage area of the trailer. "Brett never does anything half-way. He's a first-class-all-the-way kind of guy. But all this elegance is bound to make you more of a target with the less fortunate jockeys out there. Don't forget that most of them are forced to live on the backside in small, dingy one-room, hole-in-the wall apartments or out of rusty, beat up old trailers or truck campers like the one you and your dad arrived here in."

"Surely you don't think I've forgotten what that was like, or that I would flaunt all this luxury as if it actually belonged to me."

"You won't have to flaunt anything—just pulling onto the backside in this rig will broadcast you and Sonny as the target."

Olivia turned to stare at him. "You're not jealous of me having such a rig, are you?"

Justin laughed. "No. I'm not jealous. The way you and your dad have turned Sonny around and how you've taken all the bumps and bruises the past couple of days without complaining or quitting, you deserve to ride in style. I'm just still worried about what's going to happen to you on the track. Just wait until you race your first race, and then you'll know why I'm worried."

"He's right," said Jan hugging Olivia around the shoulders. "Most men think women shouldn't compete in their realms whether that's on the racetrack, in the show ring, or on the battlefield. Just be prepared for some real discrimination. No one is going to cut you any slack. If anything, they'll probably join forces against you."

"You two aren't trying to scare me out of this, are you?"

"No, of course not," said Jan. "I just don't want you to go into this thinking that you're going to be given a fair shake, because you won't. You're going to have to earn their respect, but from what I saw of you this week out here at the starting gate, you'll earn that respect in no time. It's not easy to ride a horse that shoots out of the gate like a rocket without sliding off his backside."

Olivia and Justin exchanged looks and burst out laughing.

"What's so funny?" asked Jan.

"Let's just say that I know exactly what you're talking about," said Olivia. "I even have the bruises on my backside to prove it."

"That's what you get for not following orders," said Tom as he led Bud into the horse trailer.

Olivia whipped around and glared at Justin.

Justin threw both hands up. "Don't look at me," he protested. "I didn't say a word."

"No one had to tell me anything," said Tom. "Did you actually think I wouldn't notice how gingerly you've been sitting down in a chair these past two days or how you grimaced every time you lowered yourself into the saddle? I knew you'd done something stupid the other day when I drove up to the cottage after meeting with Brett and saw you sitting on that pillow on the swing. And, by the way, you left the big bag of Epson salts next to the Jacuzzi. You're just lucky that your butt is the only thing that's sore."

"Why didn't you say something?" asked Olivia.

"Because I figured you'd already learned an important lesson, and I enjoyed watching you try to hide your discomfort." Tom leaned over and kissed Olivia lovingly on the cheek. "Okay. I think we have all the equipment and feed in the trailer. Now you'd better go and get Sonny. It's time to get him loaded and head on out of here. There's no telling how long it'll take to load him."

"I bet he'll load just fine so long as he sees Nanny and Bud are already inside," said Jan.

"I hope you're right," said Olivia remembering the horrible scene the last time someone had tried to load Sonny in their old trailer.

When she got to the barn, Sonny was already prancing

153

around nervously and obviously worrying about the disappearance of Bud and Nanny. "Come on, big fellow. There's nothing to worry about. I'm going to take you to your buddies." After she attached the lead rope to his halter, she took his head into her hands and stared deep into his eyes. "Well, this is it, my young friend. We've got a lot to prove to a bunch of folks who don't think we can do this and to some who will try to stop us. I'm counting on you to take care of me, and I promise I'll do everything I can to take care of you. We're in this together, win or lose, right?"

Sonny tossed his head and softly nickered.

"Well, okay, then. Let's go get 'em," she whispered hugging him tightly around the neck.

As Jan predicted, Sonny walked right into the trailer on the first try. Now, as they pulled away from the cottage, Olivia watched and waved through the gigantic side mirror of the truck until Justin slipped out of sight. She bowed her head and silently prayed that he wasn't also slipping out of her life. As unexpected tears flooded down her cheeks, she could still feel the warmth of his kiss on her lips.

"Dad," she mumbled. "I'm scared."

"So am I, sweetie," he muttered, reaching across the gigantic cabin of the truck to take hold of her hand. "So am I."

Chapter 22

The five-hundred and fifty mile drive from Fredericksburg, Texas to Ruidoso, New Mexico went smoothly, but Tom was relieved when they finally pulled onto the backside of Ruidoso Downs. "Come on, Olivia," he called. "We've got to get over to the track office this morning before there's a long line to get registered." He pulled open the built-in drawer under the desk in the motor home and took out the folder containing the required registration papers and licenses they needed to register with the racetrack officials.

"Coming," replied Olivia as she finished pulling her hair back and tucking it up under a ball cap. "Do you have everything we need?"

"I've got the file, and I just checked to make sure all the papers are there, so let's get going. We can't even unload the animals until we get clearance from the Race Office."

"Ok. I'm ready."

Tom turned around to look at her. "Why do you have your hair tucked up under that cap? You can't conceal the fact that you're a girl by simply hiding your hair."

"I just thought there was no sense in flaunting my femininity," she said.

Tom shook his head and laughed. "Flaunt it. Who cares?" He reached up and pulled off the ball cap from her head. "Take out that old rubber band and shake loose your curls."

157

"Seriously? I don't even wear my hair down at home," she said pulling the rubber band out of her hair and tossing her head to shake her hair loose. "You're the boss. I'm counting on you to guide me through this."

Tom opened the door of the trailer, and the intensity of the outside air hit him like a slap in the face. "Man, it's already hot out here," he said. "I've got to get those horses out of the trailer and over to the barn in a hurry."

"I opened all the vents and made sure the fans were all running. You're parked in the shade, so the animals should be okay for a little while," assured Olivia. "But you're right. We need to get all the registration taken care of before it gets any hotter."

"Nice rig," called a jogger as they walked away from the trailer. "You must have a good horse inside to afford something like that."

"We do, indeed," called Olivia as the jogger passed on by.

"Geez, Olivia, don't start with the bragging," replied Tom. He turned to get a better look at the jogger. "Do you know who that is?" he asked.

"No. Should I know him?"

"You certainly should," replied Tom, turning to look at her. "He's the top jockey in American Quarter Horse Racing."

"That was Diego Sanchez?" asked Olivia. "He holds

158

more records on more racetracks than any other jockey. Remember when we saw him last fall in Dallas? He won eight of the nine races. Of course, he was also riding on the best horses."

Tom reached out and put his arm around Olivia's shoulders. "Like I told you back home, that's how it works. When you win, you get to ride winners. You're one of the lucky jockeys out here. You don't have to beg for a ride, and you get to ride a winner as your first mount."

"I know," admitted Olivia. "I'm sure that won't help me make any friends with the other jockeys who would give their right arm to have a chance to ride a horse like Sonny."

"You've got that right," said Tom. "You should get to know Sanchez. I hear he's a nice guy. I'm sure he could help you maneuver your way into the culture here."

Together they climbed up the stairs to the Racing Office and pushed open the paneled door.

"Can I help you?" asked one of several clerks behind the counter.

"Howdy," said Olivia. "We're the Blakes. We're here to register Raven's Son and our pony horse and goat."

"Do you have your papers in order," asked the clerk, who obviously was disinterested in who they were.

Tom handed the folder of papers to the clerk and motioned for Olivia to sit down in one of the leather chairs in the waiting area. He knew it would take time for the clerk to sort through all of the documentation he had given him.

Horseracing is a highly controlled industry. A trainer can't just pull up to a racetrack, unload his horse, and enter it into any race. Each state has its own set of rules and regulations designed to protect the animals, the jockeys, and the fans. Racetrack officials require every trainer to present all the required health and tattoo information for horses and compulsory licenses and other paperwork for the trainer, owner, and jockey.

Olivia flipped through a racing magazine she found laying on the chair next to her, and Tom nervously fussed with the brim of his hat as he stood at the counter. When the official checked Olivia's license, he glanced over at her with a frown. "So you've never raced before," he commented scornfully.

"Only with local horses back at the ranch, but I've got a good horse and a good trainer, and I'm ready to win this meet," she announced proudly.

Tom frowned at her and indicated that she was to tone down her overly enthusiastic display of confidence.

"Hmm. We'll see about that," replied the official. "We don't have any women jockeys in the Futurity this year, so you'll certainly be an oddity."

"Do you have female jockeys in any of the other races?" asked Olivia.

"We've had a few in the past but none this meet. Most women don't last long in this profession. Oh, there've been a few good ones but not many."

"Well, I intend to be one of the few good ones," proclaimed Olivia. She got up and walked over to the counter as the clerk continued to stare at her.

"Oh, is that so," he laughed.

Tom bumped her with his hip and frowned down at her again. "Do you need anything else from us?" he asked the official.

"Nope, everything seems to be in order. Just make sure you show up at your scheduled time with the checkers, so we can get the required published works for the handicappers and the gate clearances we need. Good luck, young lady. If you and your horse are as good as you think you are, I'll expect to be seeing your number up on the tote board as a winner." He burst into loud laughter and slammed his fist down on the stapler to collate all of their required paperwork. He was still laughing when Tom grabbed Olivia by the sleeve and dragged her out of the office.

"Just when, Olivia, are you going to learn not to be so arrogant?" Tom shook his head and stomped down the steps.

"He started it," defended Olivia. "He was making fun of me."

"He was simply pointing out the obvious. You're a freak around here, and you'd better get used to it. You'll get a lot further with an attitude of humility than you will by walking around with a chip on your shoulder and by being so darned arrogant and cocky."

Olivia scuffed her boot in the dust and shoved her hands deep into the pockets of her jeans. "Well, it's true. I do intend to be one of the best."

"Fine," said Tom, exhaling deeply. "Let's just keep your goals to ourselves for right now. The more you spout off, the more consolidated the other jockeys will become in making sure you don't win. Your superciliousness can ruin Sonny's chances at winning. Is that what you want?"

"No, of course not."

"Then keep you grandiose thoughts to yourself, got it?"

"Got it," said Olivia appropriately chagrined.

The rest of the morning was spent transferring the animals and equipment to their assigned stalls in the barn. As they were loading the last of the hay and feed from the rig into their utility truck, Olivia suddenly stopped and turned to her dad? "Did you hear that? That's Sonny's panic whinny. Something must be wrong in the barn," she said. "Hurry. We can come back to get the rest of this stuff later."

She backed the small truck away from the van and turned it around toward the barn. "Come on, Dad. Get in," she shouted.

Tom dropped the bale of hay he was carrying and jumped

into the moving cart next to Olivia. As they approached the racing barn where Sonny was stalled with Nanny and Bud, they could hear Sonny's frantic snorting and whinnying. He appeared to be extremely agitated for some reason, and Olivia could hear him kicking at the double-dutch door. "I wonder what's wrong with him," she said stomping harder on the accelerator.

"I think I know what's bothering him," responded Tom as they turned the corner of the aisle way.

"Well, well, well. We meet again," said a man who was leaning up against Bud's stall door.

Olivia stared blankly at the menacingly looking stranger. "Do we know you?" she asked as she grabbed hold of the U-bolt on the door of Sonny's stall. "Easy Sonny," she soothed. "What is it fellow?"

The man quickly moved away as Olivia entered the stall. She grabbed Sonny by the halter and ran her hand over his neck. "He's as tense as I've ever seen him, Dad. Who are you, and what did you do to him?" she shouted at the stranger.

"Olivia, this is Doug Rickerson. Don't you remember him? He was the trainer who had Sonny before we picked him up."

"Oh, yes. Now I remember. You're the reason we had to spend most of the winter trying to..."

"What can we do for you, Mr. Rickerson?" interrupted

Tom. He shot a warning look at Olivia.

"I don't want anything," snarled Rickerson. "I just wanted to see if you'd been able to calm down this crazy horse. From the looks of things, it doesn't look like you have."

"Oh, we calmed him down, all right," said Olivia. "But it's obvious that he senses your threatening presence here, so if you don't mind, we'd appreciate it if you'd just keep your big black Stetson and shiny alligator boots away from his stall. You practically ruined this poor horse."

Shrugging his shoulders and arching his back, Rickerson jerked off his dark-tinted glasses and turned to glare at Olivia with cold, steely grey eyes. Continuing to stare at her, he slowly closed the temple pieces of his glasses together and carefully tucked them inside the pocket of his expensive looking gray, linen jacket. Before saying anything, he reached up and took off his tall, black Stetson hat and then twirled it around on his hand a couple of times, pretending to flick something off its slightly upturned brim. He then placed it carefully back on his head, covering his gray, greasy looking hair. Finally, he spoke. "I want to make myself perfectly clear to you, young lady," he began. "If I hear tell of you making any negative remarks about my training of this crazy horse, I will make sure that you, your squirrely horse, and your washed-up father never race in Quarter Horse racing again. I don't care if Brett Kendall is your rich owner. One remark from you about my training methods, and you'll likely to find yourself…"

"I wouldn't be making any menacingly threats to these nice people if I were you Doug," called out a female voice from behind them.

Tom swung around to face an attractive, middle-aged woman who was walking down the aisleway toward them. "Hello, Tom," she said starring deeply into his shocked eyes.

Olivia turned toward her father and watched as patches of red crept up his neck, transforming his cheeks to a bright shade of mulberry.

"Lillian?" muttered Tom.

"It's been a long time, hasn't it?" she responded still staring into his eyes.

"You two know each other?" asked Doug Rickerson fidgeting nervously with his hat again.

"We do," responded the woman. "Now why don't you apologize to these nice folks for your unfriendly greeting and go see about my horses."

"Right away," stammered Rickerson. "You knew I was just joking with you a bit didn't you, young lady. I'm glad to see you got this horse to settle down a little. Well now, I'll just leave y'all to get settled in. See you on the track," he called as he hurried off.

Olivia continued to stare at the beautiful, well-dressed woman. She wondered what someone like her was doing hanging around the barns at a racetrack and what her connection was to her dad. The woman's crisp, short-sleeved, linen blouse was obviously expensive, and her stylish, tan slacks looked as if they had been tailored to perfectly fit her slim figure. An expensive, thin leather belt that matched her low heel pumps encircled her tiny waist, and a huge solitaire diamond necklace sparkled from a delicate, gold chair around her neck. The light hint of expensive perfume waft through the air as she casually tossed her shoulder length, wavy blonde hair away from her face.

Tom hadn't moved a muscle since he'd stammered out the woman's name, and Olivia cleared her throat in an attempt to snap her dad out of his stupor.

The woman turned toward Olivia and offered her hand through the open stall door. "Hello, I'm Lillian Cosby, and you are Olivia, right?"

"I'm sorry," muttered Tom. "Lillian, this is my daughter, Olivia. Olivia, this is Lillian Cosby."

"It's nice to meet you," responded Olivia reaching over the stall door to shake Lillian's soft, smooth hand. *She obviously doesn't ride horses,* Olivia decided. *Her hands are as smooth as silk. I bet she's never done anything in her life to get a callous or a blister. Her French manicure is probably re-polished every day, and her gorgeous hair must be styled every morning by some famous hair designer.* She turned toward her dad, expecting him to offer some explanation of how he knew Lillian, but it was obvious that no explanation was forthcoming at the moment.

"It's nice to see you again, Olivia. The last time I saw

you, you were a tiny, little infant." Lillian then turned her attention back to Tom, who remained frozen in place. "I'm glad that you're back into training race horses, Tom. I've always wondered what happened to you after Ruidoso. You got a raw deal out of that even though you had nothing to do with that whole mess."

Tom continued to stare at her as if he were looking at a ghost from the past. Finally, he slowly shook his head and muttered, "I'm training for Brett Kendall."

"Impressive," said Lillian, "but I thought he only raced thoroughbreds."

"This is his first venture into Quarter Horse racing." He glanced over at the stall as Sonny kicked at the door again. "Well, it was nice to see you again, Lillian, but if you'll excuse us, Olivia and I have to get Sonny exercised. We just rolled in here a couple of hours ago, so we've got a lot to do before he's ready for his first schooling race."

Olivia detected a slight flinch from Lillian and noticed the stunned look on her face after her dad had so obviously dismissed her.

"Oh, sure. Well, okay, then," Lillian muttered obviously flustered by the coolness of Tom's remark. "I'd better go and check on my own horses. Maybe I'll see you again soon," she said glancing at Tom who had already turned his back and was fumbling with the buckle on Sonny's halter.

"It was nice meeting you, Mrs. Cosby," called Olivia.

Lillian stopped and looked back at her. "Please, call me Lillian. Cosby is my family name. I'm not married," she replied as she turned and hurried off.

Tom turned to watch her walk away and exhaled a deep, long sigh. "Come on, Olivia. Let's get Sonny out and walk him around for a while."

"Would you mind explaining what that was all about?" asked Olivia.

"Yes. I would mind. It's none of your concern, so drop it, and don't ask me about it again. Now go get Sonny's lead rope like I told you to."

Her dad never spoke to her in that tone of voice, and she sensed that she shouldn't push this issue with him right now, but she couldn't help but wonder what it was all about. Lillian looked like she was about the same age as her dad—maybe a year or so younger. In all their years together, Olivia had never once heard him mention Lillian's name. "Weird," she said. "I thought I knew everything about my dad." She sighed and grabbed the lead rope from the large trunk in their tack stall and hurried back to where her dad was still standing and staring blankly in the direction where Lillian had disappeared.

Chapter 23

Olivia leaned over from the saddle and handed the clocker a card with the required information for her first published run. On the card, her dad had written Sonny's registered name, her name as the jockey, and the distance to be run during the timed workout. At Ruidoso, as with other racetracks, each trainer must have a clocker check the speed of the horse over a specified distance. The clocker is an official appointed by the racetrack who uses a handheld stopwatch or some other technology to time the identified horse in a dash from the starting gate. The process determines if the horse meets the required speed index for the track or for the particular meet and provides handicapping information. Since she and Sonny were classified as first-time starters, they were required to have two published runs with company from the starting gate, which meant that they had to race against other horses during their timed trial.

"OK, missy," shouted the clocker. "You're up next. Head on over to the starting gate."

Olivia immediately felt her hands turn to ice and her whole body stiffen. This was a pivotal moment for everyone. She was well aware of the significance of looking good to the handicappers if she and Sonny were to get noticed and to be seen as serious contenders.

"Are you okay, Olivia," called Tom from his seat on the

railing. "Breathe, hang on, and just let Sonny do the work."

Olivia smiled and waved to her dad. "I've got this," she muttered in an effort to reassure herself as much as she was trying to convince her dad that she was focused and calm. "Okay, Sonny, let's show them what you can do," she said. She leaned forward to pat him on the neck. "This is it, fellow. We've got to pass the gate test, or we'll have to pack up and go home." She heaved a big sigh as she suddenly realized how crucial this moment was for everyone, not just for her and Sonny.

When they approached the starting gate, Sonny hesitated for a moment and refused to move forward. "Come on, fellow. You can't mess up here. If you don't enter the starting gate, we'll be disqualified," she whispered. She glanced over at the starting gate official and noticed that he was talking with Doug Rickerson. *What's he doing out here?* she wondered.

"Come on," called the steward, "get that horse in here. We haven't got all day."

"Will you please ask Mr. Rickerson to leave the gate area," she called out.

"He's leaving," answered the steward. "I just told him that he had no business being here. Now get your horse in the gate."

Olivia moved Sonny to the side as Doug Rickerson passed close by them, laughing at her. "Have a nice ride," he sneered.

Sonny walked straight into the gate with no problem once Rickerson was out of sight. Inside the tight space, he snorted and pawed the ground anxiously waiting for the gate to open. Olivia grabbed hold of the end of his mane and grasped it tightly in her left hand. She drew her legs in tight against Sonny's sides and leaned forward over his powerful neck. She could feel the tension building in him as he stared straight ahead. He clearly was ready to shoot out of the gate and run at breakneck speed to the finish line. He paid absolutely no attention to the other horses in the gate with him, nor did Olivia. It was obvious that he just wanted the gate to open, so he would be free to push off with his powerful hindquarters and reach out with his fully extended forelegs digging into the sandy track and propelling him forward in long, powerful strides. He loved to run, and Olivia wanted to make sure she would do nothing to get in the way of his freedom to race his race.

When the gate finally opened, Sonny burst out of it with such speed that Olivia had to grab hold of his flying mane with both hands to keep from shooting off backward. Out of the corner of her eye, she saw the horse in the gate next to her dart toward them, but Sonny was so quick that he avoided a near collision with the other horse. He flew down the track faster than Olivia had ever seen him run and left the other horses far behind to chase his dusty trail.

When they sailed past the finish line, the clocker stared down at his stopwatch. "That horse just set the meet record," he shouted. "Who in the heck is he?"

Tom ran down the track to meet Olivia as she circled back

around.

"Did you see him run," she yelled to her dad. "I've never, ever seen him run like that before, and look, he isn't even breathing hard."

"I know. I know," shouted her dad excitedly. "I was afraid you'd fall off because he was moving so fast."

As they approached the track exit gate, a throng of reporters and track regulars crowded around them, shouting questions and congratulating them on such an amazing run. Tom fielded most of the questions as he pushed through the crowd to lead Olivia and Sonny back to the barn. Above the crowd, Olivia turned around in her saddle and watched Doug Rickerson pull the jockey from the horse that almost collided with them at the starting gate. Rickerson's face was flushed, and it looked like he was about to explode as he shook and yelled at the poor jockey.

Chapter 24

Sonny performed flawlessly in the schooling races. During each of them, he lunged out of the gate and raced straight ahead at impressive speeds. In two of the three races, he had actually come across the finish line first, but on the last race, several jockeys conspired to box him in, and Olivia was unable to guide him around their barricade before the race ended. She discovered later that the jockeys involved in the blockade rode for Doug Rickerson. When she complained to her dad, he simply smiled and said, "Welcome to horseracing." However, he spent the next two weeks showing her how to anticipate a possible blocking strategy and how to maneuver Sonny around or through it.

The days and weeks passed by quickly, as they prepared Sonny to race in the trials for the Ruidoso Futurity, which was the first leg of the Quarter Horse Triple Crown. Early morning workouts, followed by cool downs, baths, and walking Sonny occupied most of Olivia's time. She and her dad intentionally stayed pretty much to themselves, away from the other jockeys and trainers. Olivia suspected that her dad was intentionally avoiding the possibility of running into Lillian Cosby. Olivia had seen her from a distance with Doug Rickerson on one occasion, but she had not stopped by the stall or the trailer since the day when her dad had so abruptly brushed her off.

The male jockeys were indifferent to Olivia. At first, they made derogatory remarks about her to one another in her presence—ignoring her, as if she wasn't actually there. But after the schooling races and news of Sonny's published times circulated among them, the insults stopped, and they simply stayed clear of her altogether. She was aware, though, that whenever she completed a scheduled workout with Sonny, the other major competitors hung around the track to watch her and privately clocked Sonny's sprints. It would take some time for the jockeys to accept her as a competitive professional, and it didn't actually bother her that she hadn't made any friends. She simply concentrated on keeping Sonny in shape for the upcoming trials.

Brett had nominated Sonny for all three of the futurities, even though the All American Futurity was their main target. Futurity races are only open to two-year-olds nominated by their owners months prior to the race. Owners pay a nominating fee and sustaining payments in advance to enroll a horse in a futurity race or competition. These fees are paid long before a horse is even trained to race. By paying the nomination and sustaining fees in advance, owners are simply betting on the potential of the young horse based upon breeding and early conformation. Many of the horses nominated for the futurity never actually race because they either didn't show the potential anticipated, or they were injured or unable to race for some other reason.

The Ruidoso Futurity was a 350 yard, Grade I race with a total purse of more than $400,000. A committee of experts from the American Quarter Horse Association ranks races on a scale from I to III, with I being the highest. Annually, a race is ranked based upon the quality of horses it attracts and its overall importance in racing. Additional requirements for graded races include minimum purse and distance specifications.

It would certainly add to Sonny's value if he could win the Ruidoso Futurity. Although the purse was substantial, Olivia realized that Brett had much more invested in Sonny. Besides, Brett would not get the whole amount of the purse. The track distributes the total purse according to predetermined percentages for each of the top five horses and a standard amount for horses coming in 6th through 10th. The owner then has to divide the purse by some predetermined ratio with the trainer and the jockey. But if Sonny could win all three futurities, as the Triple Crown winner he would bring home additional prize winnings amounting to over four million dollars. That amount of money was more than she could even imagine. She and her dad would earn a considerable fee if Sonny won the Triple Crown, but she wasn't racing for the money, although they obviously needed it. She just loved the challenge of maneuvering a powerful horse through a crowd of competitors down the 350 or 450 yards of track in just seconds. Her experience in the schooling races with Sonny clarified in her mind that being a jockey was what she wanted to do for as long as she could do it.

Every evening, she talked with Justin spending hours on video calls through Skype. She loved seeing him online, but it certainly wasn't the same as being with him on the front porch of the cabin. When her dad told her that he and Brett had decided not to bring Sonny home between the Triple Crown races, she had been devastated because that meant she wouldn't be back in Texas until September. Following the Ruidoso Futurity in late May, was the Rainbow Futurity in July, and then the All American with time trials in August and the actual running of the race on Labor Day. Justin promised that he would come out for at least one of the races, but his schedule was so tight that he wasn't sure when he could make it. She realized she had to stay focused on Sonny, but she was beginning to feel homesick, even though she didn't actually have a home to call her own.

As she was shutting down her computer, a light knock on the door of the trailer caused her to jump. She knew her dad had a key, so he wouldn't be knocking. She pulled back the drape to look out the window of her bedroom and was surprised to see Lillian Cosby standing at the front door. She quickly went to the front of the trailer to answer her knock.

"Hello, Olivia," said Lillian. She jumped backward as Olivia lost hold of the door, and it swung open almost knocking her off the first step.

"Sorry about that. I didn't realize the door would swing open so wide. My dad isn't here," said Olivia. "He went into town to pick up some supplies. I don't expect him back until late this evening."

Lillian smiled up at her. "I know he's not here. It's you that I want to talk to."

"Me?"

"May I come inside?" asked Lillian.

"Oh, sure, come on in. I'm sorry. I wasn't thinking." Olivia stepped back to let Lillian climb the steps to the entertainment room of the trailer. "Can I get you a soda or some water?"

"No. Thanks. What a beautiful trailer. You must enjoy traveling around in such style."

"Actually, this is our maiden trip," said Olivia.

"Really? Is this also your first race?" asked Lillian appearing surprised.

"Yes, for me it is."

"But not for your dad, right?"

Olivia was beginning to feel uncomfortable about the constant questioning. "You said you wanted to talk to me about something," she reminded Lillian. "Would you like to sit down?"

"Thanks, I will. I'm not sure exactly where to start." She sat down on the edge of the sofa and glanced up at Olivia.

Olivia sat across from her in one of the recliners and waited for Lillian to explain the reason for her visit.

"Well, I don't know if you're aware of it or not, but I'm the owner of a large horse farm in California. I inherited it from my dad. He died earlier this spring."

"I'm sorry about your loss. I can't imagine losing my dad," consoled Olivia.

"I'm sure you can't. The two of you seem very close. I

can't say the same about the relationship I had with my dad." Lillian hesitated for a moment and then continued. "I never knew my mother; it's just been my father and me for almost twenty years after my sister died."

"Hmm. That's the way it's been for me too."

Lillian shifted her gaze away for a moment before continuing. When she looked back at Olivia, there were tears in her eyes. "I know, Olivia. You see. I knew your mother a long, long time ago."

Olivia squirmed uncomfortably in the large recliner. "I don't know much about her. Dad never talks about her. All I know is that she died in a car accident years ago, shortly after she left me and my dad."

"Would you like to know more about her?" asked Lillian.

Olivia looked deeply into Lillian's tear-filled eyes. "I'm not sure. I probably should want to know about her, but she never seemed real to me. I don't have any memories with her in it."

Lillian took out a neatly folded tissue from the pocket of her pale yellow, silk jacket and dabbed gently at her nose and eyes. "I'm sorry," she mumbled, "allergies."

Olivia knew she was lying; those were genuine tears in her eyes. "Lillian," she whispered softly, "is there something you *want* me to know about my mother?"

Lillian carefully put the tissue back into her pocket and

smiled up at Olivia. "You sure get right to the point, don't you? You're a lot like your dad."

"Thanks. I consider that a real compliment."

Lillian stared at her for several moments and then quickly got up from the sofa and walked to the door of the trailer. "I'm sorry, Olivia. This was a mistake. I shouldn't have come here. Please, don't tell your dad I was here." She quickly opened the door and ran out before Olivia could say a word.

Olivia just sat there, transfixed and staring out the window, as Lillian's expensive, luxury car sped away and disappeared down the road leading toward the barn.

Chapter 25

Olivia could hardly wait to call Justin and tell him about the strange visit from Lillian. She was dying to tell someone about it but knew that she couldn't mention it to her dad. She glanced at her watch. Justin should be awake by now. He was still training all night, so she was careful not to call him until late afternoon. He typically slept until one or two o'clock. It was three now, and she knew he would be in his office in the training barn. She quickly logged on to SKYPE and placed a video call to him.

"Hey there," he said answering her call. "This is kind of early for our evening meeting. What's up? Is everything okay?"

"I know it's early, but I have something strange to tell you about."

"Strange? What is it? You look flushed, even on my computer screen."

"Do you remember me mentioning Lillian Cosby?"

"Sure. She was the lady that appeared at your stall the first day you got there and caused your dad to sort of freak out, right?"

"Exactly," replied Olivia. "Well, today, she showed up at the trailer and wanted to talk to me. She said she knew my dad wasn't here. It was really uncomfortable."

"Why? What did she say?"

"She said she knew my mother and asked me if I wanted to know more about her."

"And?" interjected Justin, anxious for Olivia to get to the point.

"Well, basically that's it. All of a sudden, she just jumped up from the couch and said that her coming here was a big mistake and begged me please not to tell my dad that she was here."

"Olivia, I think you just did."

"What do you mean?"

"Look behind you."

Olivia whipped around to see her dad standing behind her looking as pale as a ghost.

"I'll just hang up Olivia," she heard Justin mutter.

"How long have you been standing there, Dad? I didn't hear you come in."

"Long enough," answered Tom.

Olivia could see the disappointment and concern in her dad's eyes. "I'm sorry. Lillian asked me not to say anything to you."

"Since when have we kept secrets from one another?" he quipped.

"Evidently for twenty-years," she answered defiantly. "What does Lillian Cosby know about my mother that I don't?" She watched as all the color drained from her dad's face, and she thought he was going to faint. She jumped up and quickly thrust a glass of water at him. "Here, Dad, drink this, and then, when you're ready, tell me about the connection between Lillian Cosby and my mother. There's no sidestepping this now. I have a right to know what's going on."

Tom sat staring down into the glass of water as he swirled it around and around. Finally, he looked up at Olivia and mumbled. "She's your mother's sister."

Olivia plopped down on the sofa and sat there in a state of dazed confusion trying to process what she had just heard. Her emotions bounced around from shock to anger to sadness until they finally settled on sympathy and compassion. She got up and climbed into the large recliner with her dad. Curling up in his lap and resting her head on his shoulder, she softly whispered, "Why didn't you ever tell me about her before this?"

"It's a long, distressing story, Olivia. One that I've been running from since you were just an infant and that I hoped you would never have to hear."

Olivia waited in silence, knowing that her dad was searching for the words to tell her about what he had purposefully kept hidden from her for years.

After several minutes, he began to slowly tell her the story. "I met Lillian before I met your mother. She was friends with some of the other girls who were trying to get a ride on some of the race horses around the track. Back then, it was unheard of that a woman would be a jockey, so women would work as exercisers, pony riders, or as barn help. Lillian led me to believe that she was just one of the other girls working around the barn to earn money to buy a horse of her own. She loved horses as much as I did, and we became close friends.

When we went out, it was with a crowd of other young people who were also working around the barns. I had no idea that Lillian's father was a millionaire or that she had a younger sister. She was actually rooming with some of the other girls in a cheap apartment near the track. She was shy and unpretentious, and none of us ever suspected that she was from a wealthy family, not even the girls she lived with. Anyway, one day this gorgeous girl shows up at the barn and asks if I knew Lillian."

"So, you were actually dating Lillian before you met mom?"

"Like I said, we weren't a couple. Lillian and I were just friends, at least that's how I saw our relationship. I learned later that Lillian saw it differently. Anyway, when I met your mother, I was swept off my feet. She was young, beautiful, and impetuous, and I fell in love with her the first time we met. When she told me that Lillian had run away from home to get away from their controlling, dominating father, who was a rich businessman who dabbled in horses as a hobby, I was floored.

Lillian never said a word about her feelings for me when I started dating her sister, but she did warn me that if her father ever found out that her sister was dating a poor, start-up horse trainer, he would put an end to the relationship. So your mother and I continued to be discrete about our affair, but somehow her father found out about us. We blamed Lillian for telling him, although she denied it. She immediately left for California, deeply hurt and angry that we would accuse her of such a thing. Later, we found out that one of the young jockeys who rode for her father and who was jealous of my relationship with your mom told him. Anyway, when he learned of our affair, he immediately forbid your mother to have anything to do with me. He arranged to have her sent back to California on his private jet—only, she never went. She snuck away to my trailer, and we took off for Las Vegas to get married."

Olivia climbed out of her dad's lap and sat down on the floor, resting her head on her dad's knees. "Poor Lillian, did you ever apologize for accusing her?"

"No. I never saw her again until several years after your mother had left."

"That's too bad. What happened then between my mother and you?"

"Well, of course, her father was furious. He eventually tracked us down and ordered her to have the marriage annulled. When she refused, he told her that he never wanted to see her again, and from that day forward, he only had one daughter, Lillian."

"That must have been hard to hear from your own father," said Olivia.

Tom looked deeply into Olivia's eyes and reached out to take hold of her hand. "It was, and, of course, your mother was hurt and angry, but eventually she stopped brooding over it. We didn't have much money back then, but we managed. However, as time went on, we started having more and more arguments over money. She wanted to buy a ranch and build our own training facility, but there was just no way we could afford it. Then, when she got pregnant with you, she was delighted and stopped harping about buying a ranch. Unfortunately, shortly after you were born, it was like something snapped in her. I guess what happened to her was what they call post-partum depression. Nothing I did was good enough for her, and one day she just up and left us both. I never heard from her again until one day Lillian arrived at the Ruidoso racetrack to tell me that she had been killed in a car wreck in California. Evidently, she had made amends with her dad and had gone home."

"So Lillian was part of the mess in Ruidoso too? What happened there?"

"Well, by then, I was gaining a reputation as a good trainer and had been working for a big breeder in New Mexico. I had a horse in both the Futurity and the Derby that year and had won several smaller futurities leading up to the All American with a beautiful filly named *Shezmygal*. You had a full-time nanny, and we lived in a lovely ranch house on the breeding farm in Ruidoso. Then disaster struck again."

"You mean the death of the filly during the All American?"

"Yes. When they tested the filly for drugs, they found traces of illegal painkillers. I had never given the horse any medications because she didn't need them. There was nothing wrong with her."

Olivia watched as her father's face reddened with anger as he recalled the incident. "Who did give her the drugs? Did you ever find out?"

"Not until after my reputation had been ruined, and I had lost my training license. You see, Lillian's father told the owner of *Shezmygal* that I had a reputation for doping horses and running them when they shouldn't be run. He lied and said that I had run several of his horses into the ground."

"Why would he lie about something like that?"

"I guess he wanted to get even with me because of your mother. He told me that it was my fault that she was dead."

"How could he say such a thing? It was his fault that she was in California, not yours. She had already left us, and she died when she was with him."

"I know, sweetie, but it's hard to understand what goes through a person's mind when they are full of guilt themselves and looking for someone else to blame."

"So that's why you left horse racing and started into the rodeo?"

Tom took a long drink of water before continuing. "After the Ruidoso mess, the breeder fired me and ordered me off his property. No one else would hire me for training after that, but that's not all of the story, Olivia. You see, what Lillian had really come to Ruidoso for was to warn me that her dad was hiring lawyers to take you away from me." His voice cracked, and tears rushed down his cheeks.

"What?" screeched Olivia. "He wanted to take me away from you?"

Tom pulled a handkerchief from his back pocket and blew his nose. "Yes. I guess he was trying to get some part of your mother back by taking you away from me. Anyway, he knew that if he ruined my chances to become successful at training, then he could prove that I couldn't support you and that he could provide a better home for you. But with Lillian's help, I was able to sneak away from New Mexico before he could serve me with papers for a custody hearing. After that, we had to keep moving from place to place to stay ahead of his detectives and bounty hunters."

Olivia's eyes filled with tears. "It must have been terrible for you to have to be constantly looking after me and trying to keep him away from us."

"I was always watching over my shoulder, but the strange thing was that I always got a phone message from someone each time he or one of his henchmen arrived in the town where we were."

"Who were the messages from? Lillian?"

"The voice was always muffled, but I always suspected it was her. On one of the earlier messages, the person told me that they had arrested the groom who had actually given the shot to *Shezmygal* and that my name had been cleared. Thank goodness or I wouldn't have been able to get a license to train here in New Mexico."

"I bet it was my grandfather who paid the groom to do it, don't you?" she asserted angrily.

"I don't know. He was a treacherous person, but I have to admit, I never had a chance to really get to know him." He reached down and lifted Olivia's chin to look into her eyes. "Maybe I was selfish, Olivia. I don't know. He could have given you a very different life. I'm sorry, sweetheart. You could have had a life of luxury." Tears again flowed down his cheeks, and uncontrollable sobs racked his body.

Olivia leaped up from the floor and climbed into his lap again. "Please, Dad. Don't ever be sorry for what you have given me. I treasure the closeness and happiness that we've had together. I am so glad you kept me from that hateful old man," she sobbed.

The two of them sat in the trailer until long after nightfall, clinging to each other as if they were still afraid that someone would try to separate them.

Chapter 26

The next morning, Tom looked across Sonny's broad back at Olivia as they were giving him a soapy bath after his morning exercise. "What do you say we call Lillian and invite her over to the trailer for lunch?" he asked watching her carefully for her reaction to his suggestion.

Olivia's eyes lit up. "I'd like that a lot," she replied. "I think we owe her an apology for the way *you* treated her the other day and years ago."

Tom tossed the huge, soapy sponge into the bucket of water and turned on the hose to rinse the soap suds off Sonny. "You're right, Olivia," he admitted. "But when I saw her in the barn the other day, it brought back all the fears of having to dodge her father to keep him from snatching you away. I had no idea that he had died. He had never stopped pursuing us, even as late as last year. That's why I agreed to take Brett up on his offer. I saw your grandfather in the stands at our last rodeo in Oklahoma, and he showed up at the Kendall ranch right after we moved there. Thank god, Brett knew the whole story. He threatened to have Mr. Cosby arrested if he ever stepped foot on his property again. He even helped me file a restraining order to keep him away from you."

Olivia was stunned. "Really? I had no idea that this was going on. Anyway, once I turned eighteen, he couldn't have taken me away from you, could he?"

Tom shook his head. "Not through legal means, but he could have dangled a lot of money and opportunity in front of you."

Olivia stared at her dad. "I could never have been bought for any amount of money," she stormed. "It hurts me that you thought I could have been. Surely, you know that I love you too much to ever leave you—no matter how much money someone offered me."

Tom put his arms around her shoulders and pulled her close to him. "I know, honey. I'm sorry. I shouldn't have doubted you, but I was afraid that he could somehow convince you that it was the best thing for *me*, if you came to live with him. He was manipulative and deceitful. He would lie or do whatever it took to get you and to hurt me."

Olivia leaned over and gently kissed her dad on the cheek. "Thank goodness that's all behind us now. From what you told me last night, none of this was Lillian's fault. She was the one who helped you in Ruidoso, and I think we owe her for that. Now call her, and I'll go back to the trailer and start lunch."

~~~~~~~~~

Olivia was busy preparing the table in the trailer when she recognized Lillian's gentle tap on the door. "Come on in; the door's open," she called.

Lillian hesitantly climbed the two stairs leading up to the entertainment room. When he called her on the phone to ask her to come for lunch, Tom told her that he had explained the whole story to Olivia, but she was unsure how Olivia would feel about her. "This is awfully nice of you," she mumbled nervously. "Here, these are for you," she said handing Olivia a beautiful bouquet of fresh Bluebonnets. "I thought they would remind you of Texas."

Olivia reached out and gave her a quick hug. "Thanks, they're beautiful. How did you know I was homesick?"

Lillian smiled and relaxed a little, relieved that Olivia appeared to be glad to see her. "Can I help you with anything?" she asked.

"Nope, lunch is almost ready. Have a seat and just relax. Dad should be here any minute. He's still over at the barn making a last check on Sonny." She lifted up the blind and leaned over the kitchen sink to look out the window. "I swear he loves that horse more than me."

"No, he doesn't," Lillian quickly replied. "He loves you more than life itself. Believe me, I know that for a fact. He'd do anything for you."

Olivia turned to face Lillian and stared deeply into her soft green eyes. "I know that, Lillian. I'm just sorry that I didn't know about all he had to go through to keep us together. I guess we owe a lot to you for keeping us safe."

Lillian reached out and took hold of Olivia's hands. "I'm so sorry for the hardships that my dad caused you." Genuine sadness reflected in her eyes. "He spent the past twenty years obsessed with getting even with your dad for taking away my sister, who, he told me more than once, was his favorite daughter. I did what I could to help keep him away from the two of you, but it wasn't easy. He was a difficult man to deal with."

Olivia gently squeezed Lillian's soft hands. "It must have been hard for you being caught in the middle like that."

Lillian looked away for a moment and then turned back to Olivia, forcing herself to smile. "Well, that's all behind us now. I just hope we can start from here and build a new relationship. I would like to get to know you. You're actually living the life I always wanted to live. But when I was your age, it was almost impossible for a woman to break into the racing world."

Olivia chuckled. "It's still not all that easy. Many of the male jockeys still scorn us. Maybe it's partially because we have an easier time meeting weight limits. Because of their bone structure, men typically have to constantly fight weight gain."

"Hmm. I never thought about that, but that might be part of it," replied Lillian. "Anyway, I think it's wonderful that the Kendalls are giving you and your dad a chance to get back into racing. Your dad is a wonderful trainer," she said blushing.

"I agree," smiled Olivia glancing again out the window. "Oh, here he comes now."

"I'm sorry I'm late," said Tom, smiling at Lillian. His eyes locked on hers. "I wouldn't have blamed you, if you had turned me down."

Tears immediately filled Lillian's eyes, and she turned away from his piercing glance. "Here, Olivia," she nervously muttered as she grabbed a pitcher from Olivia. "Let me pour the tea. I can at least do that after all the work you've gone through to fix lunch."

For several moments, there was an awkward silence. Finally, Olivia couldn't stand it. "Okay, let's just clear the air," she blurted out. "We're all adults here, and what has happened in the past belongs there. I would like to hear more about you Lillian, or should I say *Aunt* Lillian?"

Lillian reached out and hugged Olivia close to her. "That would make me very happy, young lady. I've dreamed of this day for a long, long time, but I feared it would never happen." She reached her hand out to Tom, and he quickly grabbed it, raising it to his lips and gently kissing her fingers.

"Leave it to Olivia to eliminate the awkwardness. Thanks, sweetie," Tom mumbled winking at her. "What's for lunch? I'm starved."

"Something just for you—crow pie," teased Olivia.

"Very funny," responded Tom. "But she's right, I need to apologize for lots of things, Lillian. I'm sorry for all the misunderstandings between us. Hopefully, we can start up again where we left off years ago as very good friends."

Lillian smiled. "Well, that's not exactly where I left off, but

I'll settle for that as a start," she said and winked at Olivia.

Olivia placed a crisp, mixed lettuce salad that she lightly topped with a savory, balsamic vinaigrette dressing on the table for each of them. "The table looks lovely, Olivia," said Lillian. "The lime tablecloth and the colorful flowered salad plates look like spring. They add a feminine touch to the masculine look of the trailer."

"I try," said Olivia. "I haven't had much experience with this kind of thing, but thanks to the Food Network, I'm learning."

"You have to try one of her biscuits, Lillian. You'll never taste a better one," said Tom. He picked up the wired basket lined with a pink napkin wrapped around the hot, flaky biscuits and passed it to Lillian.

Lillian broke off a piece of the biscuit and put it in her mouth. "Oh, my gosh, Olivia. They just melt in your mouth. I agree with your dad. These are incredible."

"Thanks, but I want to talk more about you, Lillian," replied Olivia. "What's happening to the Rocking J since the death of your dad? I read in the *Chronicle* that it was for sale?"

"Olivia," snarled Tom. "Don't pry?"

"No, that's perfectly all right. It *is* for sale. I don't mind telling you about my current circumstances."

Through the salad, main course of lasagna, and dessert of chocolate cake, Lillian explained that her father had lost a great deal of money in the stock market and had to sell off most of the horses he had in their breeding program. Now the bank was foreclosing on the ranch because he had borrowed so heavily against it trying to recover his losses from the stock market. "Nothing seemed to go right for him during the past couple of years," she said. "So, if I can't sell the ranch by December, I'll lose everything, including most of the horses I have left."

"I'm sorry, Lillian," said Tom, reaching out and squeezing her hand. "Is there anything I can do to help you?"

"Not unless you have several million dollars you can loan me." She laughed. "But, you know, it's going to be all right. I've lived without money before, if you remember. And I can do it again. Right now, I do need a new horse trainer, though. I don't suppose you'd be interested in moving to California, would you?"

Tom stared at her for a moment before answering. "What about Rickerson?" he asked. "I assumed he was training for you." He knew he was skirting the issue about training her horses, but he could never leave the Kendalls.

"I fired him as soon as I got back to the barn the day I saw you. I've withdrawn my horses from the meet, and I'm going back to California later tonight." She looked over at Tom and tried to conceal the disappointment in her eyes. "I really only came out here because I saw your name on the list of trainers for nominated horses in the All American, but I'm glad that I also discovered what a rotten trainer Rickerson really is. One of my typically quiet horses has suddenly become skittish whenever he comes near her. I hope it isn't too late to salvage her."

"But I saw him with you the other day on the track," said Olivia.

"I know. He still has a couple of other people that he trains for, and he was making the same threat to me that he had made to you about not making any negative comments about him. I want you to be very careful when you race against any of the horses he trains. I don't trust him, and I saw what he did to your horse in the schooling races."

Tom wadded up his napkin and tossed it on the table. "If he does anything to hurt Olivia, I swear I'll kill him," he mumbled.

"I've learned that there are a lot of us that feel the same way about him, so you'll have to get in line, Tom. He's a crook, yet, he somehow manages to stay under the radar of commission investigators. We can only hope that he'll eventually trip himself up." She reached across the table and laid her hand over Olivia's dainty fingers. "Please, Olivia, be careful out there on the track. Don't do anything to jeopardize your safety or that of Raven's Son. Winning is not worth it."

Tom smiled at Lillian as if he was seeing her for the first time. "Lillian," he started, "I can't thank you enough for everything you've done to keep us safe through the years. I hope you won't be a stranger from now on."

She reached out and covered Tom's large, gnarly, suntanned hand with her delicate, soft one. "It's okay, Tom. I'd do it all again just to have the chance to see you and Olivia as happy as you are. Hopefully, I can continue to be part of your life in more pleasant ways from now on."

Olivia watched as her dad leaned over and kissed Lillian lightly on the cheek and then kissed her again, lingering longer with the second kiss.

Chapter 27

Summer flew by as Olivia and Sonny trained and participated in the major races leading to the All American Futurity. With her dad's careful attention to their preparation, they easily won the 300-yard Ruidoso Futurity in May and the 350-yard Rainbow Futurity in July finishing a full-length ahead of all contenders. In August, they also ran the fastest time in the trials for the All American Futurity. Now with the possibility that they might win the Triple Crown of American Quarter Horse Racing, their lives were turned upside down. Olivia, her dad, and Sonny became the *Cinderella* story of Ruidoso and Quarter Horse Racing. Reporters and young idols followed Olivia everywhere she went and crowded the fence rail to watch her workouts with Sonny. Newspapers across the country flashed sensational headlines in their Sports Sections such as *Raven's Son, Wonder Horse in Ruidoso*; *Young Female Jockey Demolishes All Male Contenders*; and *Trainer Returns To Seek Revenge.*

Interviews and news conferences filled most of their time away from the track, and both Olivia and Tom were beginning to feel the pressure of the possibility of winning, not only the All American Futurity, but the Triple Crown as well.

Winning the Triple Crown was an elusive accomplishment for trainers and their horses. Only one horse has ever won it since 1981. Olivia wanted desperately to be able to add Raven's Son to the history of the American Quarter Horse, but she understood the challenge she and Sonny faced. The

All American Futurity was the longest of the futurities' races, and only the very best horses and most experienced jockeys would be in the race.

Justin and Lillian provided the only relief that Olivia and Tom had. After Lillian left, Tom continued to call her every evening while Olivia talked to Justin through SKYPE. Olivia noticed that her dad seemed happier and more relaxed since their meeting with Lillian. She was glad for him and secretly hoped that their relationship would develop into more than friendship. Her dad deserved more from life after all he had been through.

As for her own life, Olivia had not seen Justin in person the entire summer. Between his competitions, her racing and workout schedule, and the distance between them, they could only see each other on the computer screen every night. But tomorrow, it would all be over. After the running of the All American Futurity, they would finally be going home, and she would be able to go with Justin to watch him compete in the Reno Futurity in November.

"Dad, I'm going to walk over to the barn and check on Sonny," called Olivia after she wasn't able to reach Justin on the phone or through the computer.

"Wait a second, and I'll come with you," he yelled. He quickly finished his conversation with Lillian and grabbed his jean jacket.

"I couldn't reach Justin tonight of all nights," complained Olivia. "He didn't mention going anyplace last night."

Tom reached over and put his arm around her shoulder. "Don't forget that he has big competitions to prepare for too."

Olivia leaned against her dad. "Still," she complained. "Tonight of all nights. He should know I would be nervous and want to talk with him."

Tom grabbed her by the shoulders and turned her so he could stare into her sad eyes. "Darlin', I'm sure there's a reason—a good reason. Right now, you need to forget about it and concentrate on tomorrow."

"Easy for you to say," said Olivia twisting free from his grip.

They continued to walk toward the barn in silence. Suddenly, Olivia stopped and stared in shock at a man running away from the barn with Nanny in hot pursuit right behind him. Without saying a word, both she and her dad broke into a fast run toward Sonny's stall.

As they reached the barn, the security guard was trying desperately to hold Sonny's stall door closed as he and Bud whinnied wildly.

"Easy, Sonny," screeched Olivia. She shoved the guard aside and reached up to grab hold of Sonny's halter. "Easy, fellow," she repeated trying to calm the out of control horse.

"What the heck is going on?" yelled Tom.

"I don't know, Mr. Blake. I was making my rounds, and

just as I came around the corner, I heard the ruckus. I saw some man bolt out of Sonny's stall being chased by the old goat. I slammed the door shut before Sonny was able to escape too, but I have no idea what's going on."

"Olivia, grab the water bucket and hay and get it out of Sonny's stall," yelled Tom as he swung up on Bud's back and charged out of the barn toward where they had seen Nanny chasing the man.

Olivia quickly grabbed Sonny's water bucket and tossed it over the top of the double Dutch door, and then yanked the hay bag off the wall throwing it out of the stall. Immediately she began surveying the stall looking for any needles, syringes, or other paraphernalia. All the while, she continued to calm the distraught Sonny. "It's okay, Sonny. It's okay," she repeated, holding on to his halter while she rubbed his neck and shoulders.

Once he began to calm down a little, she carefully ran her hands over his body and legs looking for any puncture wounds. Outside of the stall, she heard the security guard talking on his radio and was relieved to hear a voice on the other end say that they had captured the intruder. "We had to pull the old goat off of him," laughed the officer on the radio. "She was really working him over. We've called the Sheriff and have taken him into custody."

In a few moments, Tom rode up to the stall with Nanny following behind him. Olivia quickly opened Sonny's door to let Nanny in the stall. Sonny whinnied wildly and rubbed his massive head against Nanny's small one. "What happened?" yelled Olivia to her dad.

The veins on Tom's neck were bulging, and his face was bright red. The nerves in his cheek jerked, and his jaw was tightly clenched. He slammed the door shut on Bud's stall and then turned around and kicked the hay bag laying on the ground, sending it flying down the aisleway. "Those dirty, rotten, cheating, lying, no good..."

Olivia quickly shut Sonny's stall door and ran to her dad. "Dad, what is it?" she yelled, grabbing his arm. "Calm down, and tell me what's going on, please. What is it?"

The fear in her voice and eyes jarred Tom out of his raging fury. He pulled her into his arms and held her so tight that she could barely breathe. "I'm sorry, honey. I don't know what's going on. I have no idea who that guy was. I've never seen him around the barn or the track before. He wasn't carrying any ID on him and refused to answer any questions, but he was carrying a bag that contained a huge needle with a syringe full of a clear liquid. My gut is that he intended to inject whatever was in that needle into Sonny."

Olivia felt the blood rush to her face, and her heart pounded like it was trying to get out of her chest. "Rickerson," she hissed. "I know it was Rickerson."

Tom shook his head and heaved a deep sigh. "You're probably right, but unless that guy talks, there's probably no way to connect him to this. He's smart enough to hide behind a whole string of stupid jerks like that guy tonight."

A strange bleating sound from Nanny sent them both rushing back to Sonny's stall. "Nanny," yelled Olivia, quickly sliding the latch back on the door of the stall.

Nanny was lying on her side breathing heavily, and Sonny was nervously prancing around her nudging her gently with his nose. Tom knelt down beside her and cradled her head in his arms. He ran his hands over her chest. "Her heart is racing, and her body temperature feels high," he muttered. "She's not used to all that running and excitement. Come over here, and help me get her up. It's important that we keep her on her feet."

Together they struggled to get the hundred-pound goat up on her feet. "I'll hold her up, Olivia, and you call the Vet. Bring some fresh water and alfalfa in here too," ordered Tom. "Come on, old girl," he whispered to Nanny, "you're the heroine in all this drama; you can't quit on us now."

Tom continued to hold Nanny up, while Olivia tried to massage the goat's chest, back, and legs. Sonny never took his eyes off Nanny and continued to constantly nicker to her. When the grounds Vet finally arrived, he immediately began to hydrate Nanny and gave her medication to slow her racing heart. After several hours, she was able to stand on her own and began to wobble about the stall. The Vet also checked Sonny for any visible indication that he had been drugged.

"He looks all right," said the Vet. "He's such a beautiful horse. I can't understand why anyone would ever want to harm him." He closed up his bag and headed out of the stall. "Good luck, young lady," he said turning to Olivia. "You've caused a lot of excitement around here this summer. I hope it all pays off for you tomorrow. I have a ticket on you to win," he said smiling at her.

"Thanks," muttered Olivia, trying to muster enough energy to return his smile. After he left, she stood up, stretched her arms over her head and bent from side to side at the waist.

"Olivia, I want you to go back to the trailer. It's late, and you have to try and get some rest."

"What about you, Dad?" she asked.

"I'm going to spend the night here in the stall. I want to watch Nanny and make sure that no one else tries to get near Sonny. I don't want to relive the horror of my last American Futurity race."

Chapter 28

Olivia tossed and turned all night and was awake before dawn. She quickly made some fresh coffee and warmed up some left over biscuits in the microwave. She packed them and some honey in a small basket and rushed to the barn to check on her dad and the animals.

"Good morning, sweetie," Tom called. "Ah, you're an angel," he said as he reached for the basket.

"How's Nanny?" Olivia asked. She peered over the top of the stall door at the sleeping goat curled up next to Sonny.

"Seems to be fine," mumbled her dad with a mouthful of biscuits and honey. "She's a tough old goat."

"She is," agreed Olivia. "I just wish she could talk, so she could tell us what happened. Did you have any more visitors last night?"

Her dad blew across the top of his coffee. "Nope. Quiet all night," he answered.

"Did you get any sleep at all?" she asked.

"A little but I can sleep for a week after we get home." He smiled and took a loud sip of the coffee. "How about you? Hopefully you were able to get some rest."

"I slept sort of fitfully all night, but I feel fine this morning. I had a good dream, though," she said with sparkling eyes.

"Is it bad luck to tell your dreams?"

"I don't believe in bad luck," said Tom. "I don't believe in good luck either," he added. "Life throws some curves, and you either hit them out of the ball park, or you let them strike you out. It's all about what you do with your ups and downs; luck is not a factor in life."

"Hmm. You're being terribly philosophical so early in the morning. Anyway, I dreamed I was standing inside the Ruidoso Horse Hall of Fame, and I was telling a little boy standing next to me about the giant picture of the horse in one of the exhibits."

"And who was the horse in the picture?" asked her Dad.

"That's the odd part. I appeared to know all about the horse except its name, and even though I tried, I couldn't see the name on the plaque or see the horse's face. Crazy, huh?"

"Well, I think we both know who that horse was," said her Dad, giving her a quick hug. He turned toward Sonny's stall and laughed as both Bud and Sonny had appeared at their respective doors and Nanny's horns were barely visible next to Sonny. "They obviously heard your voice and are anticipating their morning treat."

"Good morning, fellows, and my dear lady," said Olivia reaching in her pocket for peppermints. She was certainly glad to see Nanny up and about. Opening the door to Sonny's stall, she got down on her knees and hugged the old goat around the neck. "Thanks, Nanny. You were the superhero in our saga last night, but I think if you're going to take on such a role, we need to start you on an exercise regimen to increase your stamina. I don't want any more scares from you like last night."

Nanny bleated softly and grabbed the peppermint from Olivia's outstretched hand.

The rest of the morning was spent preparing Sonny for the race and fielding questions from dozens of reporters about last night's episode and today's prediction. As the time got closer for the race, Tom paced around the barn, reminding Olivia of things he had told her dozens of times before. Finally, it was time for her to report to the jockey quarters for the weigh-in and rule review.

Before heading to the jockey's room, she went back to the trailer alone and slipped on the special riding suit sent by the Kendalls just for today's race. She stared at herself in the mirror inside the trailer. "It's hard to believe that it's all about to be over," she muttered. Soon she would be back home away from all of the hubbub and confusion for a while. The months of training, the bumps and bruises, and the tears and arguments were just memories. And all that time was spent to prepare her for today's brief dash down the racetrack for less than 20 seconds.

Though the other races were important, this was the race that they had come to Ruidoso to win. This was the big one. This was the one that could rocket Sonny and the Kendalls into the American Quarter Horse Hall of Fame. This was the one that had gotten away years ago from her dad and for years had kept him from what he loved doing most in the world. And this was the one that would give her the status she craved as a professional jockey. She drew in a deep breath and headed over to the Jockey Room.

When she got back to the barn after the weigh in, her Dad was already walking Sonny around and talking to him as if he were human. Although Olivia couldn't hear what he was saying, she could tell by the look on her dad's face that he was pleading with Sonny to keep her safe.

Unlike the other trainers, they had no extra grooms to help them ready Sonny. Although Brett had told them to hire someone, Tom wanted to do everything himself this time. He wanted to make sure that every strap, every stirrup, and every blinker was properly fitted so Sonny would be comfortable, and Olivia could safely stay on him as they dashed out of the gate.

"Are you going to be okay, Dad," she asked as she was helping to saddle Sonny.

"Olivia, don't tighten the girth so tight," he shouted. He was obviously unaware that she had asked him a question. "Sonny needs to be able to breathe comfortably."

She glanced over at him and smiled. "You look nervous," she said teasingly. "I thought I was the one who was supposed to be a nervous wreck."

"Your daughter isn't being sent to the wolves," he muttered. "Mine is. I have a right to be more nervous than you are. Everyone is going to be out to beat you today." He drew in a long, deep breath. "Well, this is what we came here for. Are you sure you don't want to change your mind? We can always scratch. All you have to do is say the word."

"Dad, I'm ready. Like I told you back home, I was born ready for this," she assured him.

"OK then, up you go, sweetheart," he said, cupping his hands for her to step into them and to be lifted into the saddle.

"Wait, wait," yelled a familiar voice from behind them.

Tom and Olivia turned around to see Justin pushing and shoving his way through the packed barn area.

"Justin! What are you doing here?" shouted Olivia, running to meet him. "I had no idea you were coming. Oh, I'm so glad you're here," she squealed jumping into his outstretched arms.

Justin picked her up and swung her around and then gently put her down, holding her at arm's length in front of him. "You look like a real jockey. The blue silks match your eyes." He leaned toward her and gently kissed her on the cheek. "That's for good luck. I hope it won't make you more nervous by us being here, but I wasn't about to miss this. I wanted to make sure I was in your famous photo at the Winner's Circle. We planned to be here all along and surprise y'all. We'd have been here earlier, but Jan had to stop twice on the way here from the airport to go to the bathroom. They're coming right behind me. Brett wouldn't let her run to keep up with me. He babies her so much that he's practically smothering her and everyone around her."

"How far behind you did you say Jan and Brett were?" asked Tom. "We have to be in the paddock in time for the post parade, or we may be scratched."

"Relax, Dad. Here they come. We have plenty of time," soothed Olivia.

Jan stumbled over a rock as they came around the corner of the barn,and Brett quickly grabbed her by the arm. "Be careful, for heaven's sake, Jan. Slow down. You're not running a race."

"Hey, y'all," called Jan. "Sorry to be arriving so late, but it's baby Brett's fault. He's scrunching my bladder." She reached out and gave Olivia a quick hug. "You look perfect, Olivia. The colors suit you."

Tom glanced at his watch again. "Well, we'd better be heading over. Do y'all want to walk over with us?"

"I'm just going to take Jan over to the box seats. You guys go on. Bring him home in style, Olivia," said Brett giving her a quick hug. "Just keep yourself safe," he whispered in her ear.

Olivia smiled. "Don't you worry. Sonny and I are going to be just fine."

"Come on, Olivia," yelled Tom.

"Relax, Dad. You're going to have a heart attack if you don't calm down and breathe. Look at Sonny. He's not nervous, and neither am I," she said stepping into his cupped hands and settling herself into the saddle.

"That's because you two don't have enough sense to worry," he grumbled.

Justin reached up and patted her on the boot. She glanced down at him and smiled. "Aren't you going to come with us to the paddock?"

"Nope. I think this is a special time for you and your dad. Good luck, and stay in the saddle. Sonny will do the rest." He smiled and jogged off to catch up with Brett and Jan.

~~~~~

It was a thrill being in the post parade and sitting atop the most beautiful creature in the pack. Olivia couldn't help but notice that the reporters were snapping more pictures of her and Sonny than of the other horses. "I hope all this attention doesn't make Sonny nervous," she yelled down to her dad.

"Can't you tell? He's a cool as if he'd been doing this for years," answered Tom. "I'm the one doing all of the sweating."

Sonny snorted and bumped him with his head as if he were laughing at Tom's nervousness. Olivia leaned forward and patted Sonny on the neck. There was one thing she was absolutely certain of—none of the other jockeys knew their horses as well as she knew Sonny. They had formed a true partnership, and she trusted him to race his heart out for her. If only the other jockeys would give them a fair break, Sonny would certainly become the giant picture in the Ruidoso Horse Hall of Fame.

Chapter 29

"And they're almost all in the gate. Only two more horses to go," blasted the voice on the loudspeaker. "All eyes are on Raven's Son coming out of the No. 6 hole and his petite, female jockey, Olivia Blake. This is the big race for both horse and jockey."

Inside the gate, Olivia sucked in a deep breath and glanced up toward the sky. "Please, just keep us safe," she muttered.

"You're going to need all the help you can get," shouted the jockey next to her.

"Ah, shut up," yelled another jockey at the end of the row. "If you don't give her a fair shake, I'm going to file a complaint with the Commissioner."

Olivia glanced down the row of stalls and recognized Diego Sanchez. He smiled back at her and touched his whip to the brim of his cap. "Go get 'em tiger," he called to her.

"Women don't belong on the racetrack," shouted the jockey next to her again.

Olivia shot him a hateful glance and recognized him as one of Rickerson's jockeys who had blocked her during the schooling race that Sonny lost. *Don't think about losing, Olivia,* she reprimanded herself. *Concentrate on winning.* She reached out to grab a handful of Sonny's mane.

Everything her dad had told her swirled through her mind as jumbled words. She tightened her grip on the reins and once again sucked in a deep breath. This was their big day; their chance to prove that they belonged on the racetrack with some of the top Quarter Horses and jockeys in the business. This is what she and her dad had worked for. "Oh, dear God, please don't let me screw this up," she whispered.

"They're all in the gate, and there they go," echoed across the racetrack through the loud speakers. "Raven's Son is late leaving the gate. This can't be good for their chances at the Triple Crown."

"What is she doing?" yelled Justin. "Why didn't she break with the rest of them?"

"Perfect, Olivia," yelled her dad. "Now let him run."

"Now," yelled Olivia loosening the reins and letting Sonny shoot out of the gate. As her dad had predicted, the two jockeys on each side of her intentionally merged into her lane and formed a blockade to obstruct her run. But with the split-second delay from the gate, she was able to dart behind the horse on her left and slide Sonny into the lane vacated by one of the other jockeys. She heard the two conspirators curse as she sped down the track leaving them behind to choke on Sonny's dust.

Now it was all up to Sonny. His speed and his drive would determine whether the momentary delay in the gate was the right move. He was trailing the remaining seven horses, but he continued to surge forward, digging and pushing faster and faster with tremendous thrusts and pulls from his powerful legs. With each extended stride, he stretched as far as his body would allow, covering the ground in giant, effortless leaps and drawing closer and closer to the pack of horses ahead of them. Olivia reached out, grabbed another hunk of Sonny's mane, and crouched lower in the saddle pushing her weight forward to prevent any possible drag that her body would cause. Horse after horse fell behind them as Sonny's tremendous speed pushed him forward.

For Tom, time seemed to stand still. The noise and shouts of the announcer and of those around him were nothing but scrambled bits of static, drowned out by the loud beating of his heart. He watched, but didn't see; he heard, but couldn't understand. And then, it was over. *Where is Olivia*, he wondered. *Did we win?*

"If I hadn't seen it with my own eyes, I would never have believed it," shouted the breathless announcer. "Coming from behind to cross the finish line in just 14.9 seconds, Raven's Son just set a new race record. What a horse! What a ride! He just rode right into history as the second horse to ever win the Triple Crown."

"Oh my god," shouted Justin. "She did it; she did it." He grabbed Jan and hugged her. "Did you see that? They were absolutely flying down that track." He turned and glanced over at Tom, who was as white as a sheet with tears streaming down his cheeks. "You did it, man. You two are amazing; simply amazing."

Reality finally penetrated his stupor, and Tom took off at a run toward the track. "We did it," he shouted as he ran to meet Olivia. "We actually did it."

"I can't believe it," cheered Jan, jumping up and down.

Brett quickly grabbed her by the shoulders. "Settle down, Jan. Don't be jumping up and down like that," he yelled.

"Oh, for Pete's sake, Brett. Stop worrying about the baby and enjoy the moment. C'mon you guys. We get to go to the Winner's Circle."

Olivia struggled to turn Sonny around to head back to the finish line. He was obviously not aware that the race was over. A young girl on one of the pony horses raced up to them and reached out to grab hold of Sonny's bridle to help slow him down. "You were remarkable," shouted the girl. "You've just become the idol of every female who ever wanted to be a jockey," she yelled and smiled broadly at Olivia.

Olivia stared blankly at the young woman. Her mind was whirling and, like Sonny, she was still in race mode. The fifteen second run was a blur in her mind. The only things she remembered were counting to three and the exhilaration of flying past other horses that appeared to be nothing more than a series of blurs. "Did we really win?" she shouted to the young girl.

"Not only did you win, you set a track record. Enjoy the Winner's Circle," she said as she let loose of Sonny and rode off.

"Nice ride," yelled Diego Sanchez as he rode past her.

214

"Don't ever let anyone tell you that you don't belong on the racetrack, because you do."

Olivia could only smile. She was still trying to take it all in. When she finally arrived back at the finish line, her dad ran out onto the track and grabbed hold of Sonny's bridle. "I'm so proud of you," he said looking up at Olivia with his cheeks still wet from tears of joy and relief. "You rode him just right. No one could have ridden him any better."

"That was the longest three count of my life," shouted Olivia still trying to catch her breath after the incredible ride. "It was really hard to hold Sonny back. He wanted to charge immediately from the gate, but you were right. The brief pause let us swerve away from the two Rickerson jockeys into another lane, and Sonny did the rest. All I did was try to hold on."

"Speaking of Rickerson," Tom yelled as he tried to hold on to Sonny on the way to the Winner's Circle, "I saw some police officers lead him away just before the race."

"Good," said Olivia. "Maybe today he won what he had coming to him too. This win is for you, Dad," she said blowing him a kiss as they walked into the celebration in the Winner's Circle. When she spotted Justin, she jumped down from the saddle straight into his arms.

"You are an amazing jockey," he shouted swinging her around. "I'm so proud of you." He gently lowered her to the ground, took her face in his hands, and passionately kissed her.

Jan squeezed past the two young lovers to pull Sonny's proud head toward her. "You did it, little guy," she whispered in his ear. "I knew you had it in you from the start."

Sonny responded by lifting his head toward the sky and blasting out a loud, earsplitting whinny.

Jan laughed. "No doubt about it; you most certainly *are* Raven's son."

Keep Your Eyes On Heaven

One day when I was just a child,
I climbed on daddy's knee.
No matter what I thought was wrong,
He'd make it right for me.
"What's wrong today, my little one,"
He asked and held me tight.
"Please tell me all about it,
And I'll try to make it right."

I asked why bad things happen,
To people who are good,
And asked why things don't seem to go,
The way I think they should.
He sat real still for just awhile,
And then he sang to me,
A song that I still sing today,
When life's a mystery.

Keep your eyes on Heaven,
You don't need to know why.
Keep your eyes on Heaven,
And you'll know by and by.
Keep your eyes on Heaven,
Put your trust in God's hand.
Keep your eyes on Heaven,
He has a plan.

That little song, he sang to me
In his calm and loving way
Still lingers deep within my heart
And guides me every day.
I've learned that life's not easy,
And sometimes things go wrong

But when they do, I look up
And sing this special song

Keep your eyes on Heaven.
You don't need to know why.
Keep your eyes on Heaven,
And you'll know by and by.
Keep your eyes on Heaven,
Put your trust in God's hand.
Keep your eyes on Heaven,
He has a plan.

©Mary Lee Peck